PENGUIN BOOKS

THE TIGERS OF SUBTOPIA
and other stories

Julian Symons made a reputation before the Second World War as the editor of *Twentieth-Century Verse*, a magazine which published most of the young poets outside the immediate Auden circle. He has since become a celebrated writer of crime fiction and is also recognized as the greatest British expert on the genre. His history of the form, *Bloody Murder*, was called by Len Deighton 'the classic study of crime fiction', and was awarded the Mystery Writers of America Edgar Allan Poe Award in 1977. He has also written extensively about real-life crime in *A Reasonable Doubt* and *Crime and Detection from 1840*, and has written many articles on the historical background of both real and fictional crime. In 1976 he succeeded Agatha Christie as the President of the Detection Club, and was made a Grand Master of the Swedish Academy of Detection in 1977. He was created a Grand Master of Mystery by the Mystery Writers of America in 1982. Mr Symons also has quite a separate reputation as a biographer and as a social and military historian. In 1975 he was made a Fellow of the Royal Society of Literature. His recent crime novels include *The Blackheath Poisonings*, *Sweet Adelaide* and *The Detling Murders*. Several of his books are published in Penguins.

JULIAN SYMONS

THE TIGERS OF SUBTOPIA

and other stories

PENGUIN BOOKS

Penguin Books Ltd, Harmondsworth, Middlesex, England
Penguin Books, 40 West 23rd Street, New York, New York 10010, U.S.A.
Penguin Books Australia Ltd, Ringwood, Victoria, Australia
Penguin Books Canada Ltd, 2801 John Street, Markham, Ontario, Canada L3R 1B4
Penguin Books (N.Z.) Ltd, 182-190 Wairau Road, Auckland 10, New Zealand

This collection first published in Great Britain by Macmillan London Ltd 1982
First published in the United States of America by The Viking Press 1983
Published in Penguin Books 1984

'The Tigers of Subtopia' and 'A Theme for Hyacinth' were first published in *Ellery Queen's Mystery Magazine*, 1967 (the former as 'The Tiger's Stripe'). 'Love Affair' was first published in *Ellery Queen's Mystery Magazine*, 1968. 'Somebody Else' was first published in *Winter's Crimes 1*, Macmillan, 1969. 'The Last Time' was first published in *Winter's Crimes 3*, Macmillan, 1971. 'The Flowers that Bloom in the Spring' was first published in *Ellery Queen's Mystery Magazine*, 1979. 'The Flaw' was first published in *Winter's Crimes 11*, Macmillan, 1979. 'The Dupe', 'The Murderer', 'The Boiler' and 'The Best Chess Player in the World' were first published in this collection, 1982.

Grateful acknowledgement is made to the following for permission to reprint copyrighted material. Harcourt Brace Jovanovich, Inc.: Three lines from 'The Waste Land' from *Collected Poems 1909–1962* by T. S. Eliot, Alfred A. Knopf, Inc.: A selection from 'Le Monocle de Mon Oncle' from *The Collected Poems of Wallace Stevens* by Wallace Stevens.

Made and printed in Great Britain by
Richard Clay (The Chaucer Press) Ltd,
Bungay, Suffolk

To Daniel James Symons

Contents

The Tigers of Subtopia

It began with the telephone call from Miriam. 'Bradley,' she said, 'there are some boys outside.'

Bradley Fawcett recognized in his wife's voice the note of hysteria that was occasionally discernible nowadays. It's the menopause, Dr Brownlow had said, you must be patient with her. So now his voice took on a consciously patient tone, a talking-to-Miriam tone it might have been called, although he did not think of it in that way.

'Friends of Paul's, you mean?'

'No. Oh, no. Beastly boys. Louts. They took his sweets.'

'Took his sweets,' Brad echoed stupidly. He stared at the contract on the desk in front of him.

'They asked him for them and he gave them one or two, and then they knocked them out of his hand.' She ended on a rising note.

Had she telephoned the office simply to tell him this? Patiently he said, 'Calm down now, Miriam. Is Paul upset?'

'No, he's – but they're outside, you see, they're still outside.' There was a sound that could have been interpreted as a kind of tinkling crack and then he heard her shriek, 'They've broken the glass!'

'What glass?'

'The living room – our beautiful living-room window.'

Brad put down the telephone a couple of minutes later, feeling hot and angry. He had not rung the police because they would have come round and talked to Miriam, and he knew that would upset her. The window itself was not important, although he would have to put in a large and expensive sheet of plate glass, but this was not the first trouble they had had with hooligans in The Oasis.

Geoff Cooper's garage wall had been daubed one night with filthy phrases, and on another occasion the flowers in the middle of one of the green areas had been uprooted and strewn around as though by some great animal; on a third occasion the sandpit in the children's playground had been filled with bits of broken glass, and one little boy had cut his foot quite badly.

It was the senselessness of such acts that irritated Brad, as he said to his companions in the train, on the way back from the city to Dunkerley Green. The journey was a short one, no more than twenty minutes, but there were four of them who always made it together. The trains they caught–the 9:12 in the morning and the 6:18 at night–were never crowded, and they preferred the relaxation of sitting in the train to the tension of driving through the traffic.

Geoff Cooper, Peter Stone, and Porky Leighton all lived in The Oasis, and they had other things in common. Cooper was an accountant, Stone ran a travel agency, Porky Leighton was in business as a builder's merchant, and Brad himself was one of the directors of an engineering firm. They all dressed rather similarly for going into the city, in suits of discreet pinstripe or of plain clerical grey. Porky, who had been a rugger international in his youth, wore a striped tie, but the neckwear of the other three was sober.

They all thought of themselves as professional men, and they all appreciated the civilized amenities of life in The Oasis. Brad, who had passed the age of fifty, was the oldest of them by a decade. He liked to feel that they looked to him for counsel, that he was the elder statesman of their little group. He felt the faintest twinge of annoyance that it should have been Geoff Cooper who mentioned the idea of a Residents' Committee. The others took it up so enthusiastically that it seemed incumbent on him to express doubts.

'Forgive me for saying it, Geoff, but just how would it help?'

'Look, Brad, let's start from the point that we're not going to put up with this sort of thing any longer. Right?' That was Porky. He wiped his red face with a handkerchief, for it was hot in the carriage. 'And then let's go on to say that the police can't do a damned thing to help us.'

'I don't know about that.' Brad was never at ease with Porky. It seemed to him that there was an unwelcome undercurrent of mockery in the man-to-man straightforwardness with which Porky spoke to him.

'You know what the police were like when Geoff had that trouble with his garage wall.'

'Told me that if I could say who'd done it they would take action.' Geoff Cooper snorted. 'A lot of use that was.'

'The fact is, The Oasis is a private estate and, let's face it, the police don't mind too much what happens. If you want something done, do it yourself, that's my motto.' That was Porky again.

'Half the trouble is caused by television,' Peter Stone said in his thin fluting voice. 'There are programmes about them every night, these young toughs. They get puffed up, think they're important. I saw one this week – do you know what it was called? *The Tigers of Youth.*'

Geoff snorted again. Porky commented. 'You can tame tigers.'

'Nevertheless,' Brad said. It was a phrase he often used when he wanted to avoid committing himself.

'Are you against it? A Committee, I mean,' Geoff asked.

'I believe there must be some other way of dealing with the problem. I feel sure it would be a good idea to sleep on it.'

Did he catch an ironic glance from Porky to the others? He could not be sure. The train drew into Dunkerley Green. Five minutes' walk, and they had reached The Oasis.

There were gates at the entrance to the estate, and a sign asking drivers to be careful because children might be playing. There were green strips in front of the houses, and these strips were protected by stone bollards with chains between them. The houses were set back behind small front lawns, and each house had a rear garden. And although the houses were all of the same basic construction, with integral garages and a large through room that went from front to back, with a picture window at each end, there were delightful minor differences – like the basement garden room in Brad's house, which in Geoff's house was a small laundry room, and in Porky's had been laid out as a downstairs kitchen.

Brad's cousin, an architect from London, had once burst into a guffaw when he walked round the estate and saw the bollards and chains. 'Subtopia in Excelsis,' he had said, but Brad didn't really mind. If this was Subtopia, as he said to Miriam afterwards, then Subtopia was one of the best places in England to live.

He had expected to be furiously angry when he saw the broken window, but in fact the hole was so small, the gesture of throwing a stone seemed so pathetic, that he felt nothing at all. When he got indoors, Miriam was concerned to justify her telephone call. She knew that he did not like her to phone him at the office.

'I told them to go away and they just stood there, just stood laughing at me.'

'How many of them?'

'Three.'

'What did they look like?'

'The one in the middle was big. They called him John. He was the leader.'

'But what did they –'

'Oh, I don't know,' she said impatiently. 'They all looked the same – you know those ghastly clothes they wear, tight trousers and pointed shoes. I didn't go near them. I called out that I was going to phone the police, and then I came in and spoke to you. Why should they *do* such a thing, Bradley, that's what I don't understand.'

She was the only person who called him by his full Christian name, and he had sometimes thought that it typified the nature of their relationship, without knowing quite what that meant. It always seemed, too, that he talked rather more pontifically than usual in Miriam's presence, as though she expected it of him.

'It's a natural youthful impulse to defy authority,' he said now. 'And when you told them you were going to call the police – why, then they threw the stone.'

She began to cry. It did not stop her talking. 'You're making it sound as if *I* were in the wrong. But I did nothing, *nothing!*'

'Of course you're not in the wrong. I'm just explaining.'

'What harm have we ever done to them?'

'No harm. It's just that you may find it easier if you try to understand them.'

'Well, I can't. And I don't *want* to understand.' She paused, and said something that astonished him. 'Paul knows them. They're his friends.'

That was not strictly true, as he discovered when he talked to Paul. They sat in the boy's bedroom, which was full of ingenious space-saving devices, like a shelf which swung out to become a table top. Paul was sitting at this now, doing school work. He seemed to think the whole thing was a fuss about nothing.

'Honestly, Dad, nothing would have happened. We were playing around and Fatty knocked the sweets out of my hand, and it just so happened that Mum had come to the door and saw it. You know what she's like – she let fly.'

'Fatty? You know them?'

'Well, they come and play sometimes down on the common, and they let us play with them.'

The common was a piece of waste ground nearby, on which Paul sometimes played football and cricket. There was no provision in The Oasis for any kind of ball game.

'Are they friends of yours?'

Paul considered this. He was a handsome boy, rather small for his thirteen years, compact in body and curiously self-contained. At least, Brad thought it was curious; he was intermittently worried by the fact that he could not be sure what Paul was thinking.

Now, after consideration, Paul replied, 'I shouldn't say friends. Acquaintances.'

'They don't sound like the sort of boys your mother and I would welcome as your friends.' Paul said nothing to this. 'You were playing with them this afternoon?'

It was all wrong, Brad felt, that he should have to drag the information out of Paul by asking questions. A boy and his father should exchange confidences easily and naturally, but it had never been like that with them.

By direct questioning, of the kind that he felt shouldn't be necessary, he learned that they had been playing football. When they had finished these three boys walked back with Paul to The Oasis. On the way Paul had bought the sweets. Why had they walked back? he asked. Surely they didn't live in Dunkerley Green? Paul shook his head.

'They live in Denholm.'

Brad carefully avoided comment. Denholm was a part of the city that he had visited only two or three times in his life. It contained the docks and a good many factories, and also several streets of dubious reputation.

It would have been against Brad's principles to say that he did not want his son going about with boys from Denholm. Instead, he asked, 'Why did they come up here with you? I don't understand that.' Paul muttered something, and Brad repeated rather sharply, 'Why, Paul, why?'

Paul raised his head and looked his father straight in the face. 'John, said, "Let's have another look at Snob Hill".'

'Snob Hill,' Brad echoed. 'That's what they call The Oasis?'

'Yes. He said, "Let's see if they've put barbed wire round it yet".'

'Barbed wire?'

'To keep them out.'

Brad felt something – something that might have been a tiny bird – leap inside his stomach. With intentional brutality he went on, 'You live here. On Snob Hill. I'm surprised they have anything to do with you.'

Paul muttered again, so that the words were only just audible.

'They think I'm okay.'

Brad gripped his son's shoulder, felt the fine bones beneath his hand. 'You think it's all right for them to throw stones, to break windows?'

'Of course I don't.'

'This John, what's his last name?'

'Baxter.'

'Where does he live?'

'I don't know.' Paul hesitated, then said, 'I expect he'll be in The Club.'

'The Club?'

'They go there most nights.'

'Where is it?'

'East Street.'

A horrifying thought occurred to Brad. 'Have you been there?'

'They say I'm too young.' Paul stopped, then said, 'Dad.'

'Yes?'

'I shouldn't go there. It won't do any good.' With an effort, as though he were explaining, saying something that made sense, he added, 'You won't like it.'

In the time that it took to drive to Denholm, the bird that had been fluttering in Brad's stomach had quieted down. He was, as he often said, a liberal with a small 'l'. He believed that there was no problem which could not be solved by discussion round a table, and that you should always make an effort to see the other fellow's point of view.

The trip by car gave him time to think about his own attitude, and to admit that he had been a bit unreasonable. He could understand that these boys held a sort of glamour for Paul, could even understand to a certain extent their feelings about The Oasis. And just because he understood, it would be silly, it would even be cowardly, not to face them and talk to them.

Much of Denholm was dark, but East Street blazed with neon light. There seemed to be a dozen clubs of various kinds, as well as several cafes, and he had to ask for The Club. He did so at first without success, then a boy giggled and said that he was standing almost in front of it.

As Brad descended steps to a basement and advanced towards a wall of syncopated sound, he felt for the first time a doubt about the wisdom of his mission.

The door was open, and he entered a low-ceilinged cellar room. At the far end of it four boys were singing or shouting on a raised platform. In front of him couples moved, most of them not holding each other, but gyrating in strange contortions that he had never seen before except in one or two television programmes.

The atmosphere was remarkably clear. Well, at least most of them are non-smokers, he thought, and was pleased that he hadn't lost his sense of humour. He spoke to a boy who was standing by a wall.

'Can you tell me where to find John Baxter?'

The boy stared at him, and Brad repeated the question.

'John?' The boy gave Brad a long deliberate look, from face to shoes. Then somebody tapped Brad's shoulder from behind. He turned to face a fat boy wearing a purple shirt, jeans, and elastic-sided shoes.

The fat boy muttered something lewd.

His other shoulder was tapped. A boy with bad teeth grinned at him. 'You want the john?'

The first boy, not the fat one, tapped him, repeating the lewd remark.

The fat boy tapped him again. 'It's just looking at you. This way.' He walked slowly round Brad, staring at him. ' 'Cause we never seen nothing so square before, get it?'

As Brad looked at the clothes of the three boys around him, clothes that were different in several ways and yet were identical in the brightness of their shirts, the tightness of their jeans, and the pointedness of their shoes, he had the ridiculous feeling that it was he and not they who was outraging orthodoxy, that his neat dark suit and well-polished square-toed shoes were badges of singularity, the clothing of an outlaw.

The sensation lasted for only a moment. Then he shouted – he had to shout, because the tribal music rose suddenly to a louder beat – 'I want John Baxter.'

The boy with the bad teeth tapped him. 'You ask for the john, then you don't pay attention. I don't like that, not polite. I'm John.'

Brad faced him. 'You are? You're the John who —'

The fat boy said, 'You heard that, he said you're the john. You going to take that?'

The three of them had closed in so that they were now almost touching him, and he thought incredulously: they're going to attack me. Then a voice said, 'Break it up, come on now, break it up.'

The three boys moved back, and a stocky man with

thick eyebrows and arms like marrows said, 'Whatcher want?' Brad found it hard to speak. The man went on, 'They're blocked. You don't want to get mixed up with 'em when they're blocked.'

'Blocked?' It was a new country, a new language.

'I'm here if there's trouble, but they're no trouble – it's you that's making trouble, mister.'

'I didn't – that's not true.'

'So they're blocked, they feel good, have fun, what's the harm? You don't belong, mister. They don't like you, so why don't you just get out?'

He could just hear himself say *all right, all right.* Then there was a small scream from the dance floor, and a girl cried, 'He hit me!' The bouncer began to push his way through the crowd on the dance floor.

Brad stumbled away, eager to go, and had almost reached the outer door when there was one more tap on his shoulder. He turned again, putting up his fists. A tall dark boy he had not seen before asked, 'Want me?'

The boy was dressed like the others, but there was something different about him – a kind of authority and even arrogance.

'You're John Baxter?'

'What do you want?'

Behind him was the fat boy who said now, with a hint of silly irrational laughter in his voice, 'He says he wants John, see, so we're —'

'Shut it, Fatty,' the dark boy said. The fat boy stopped talking.

'I'm Bradley Fawcett.'

'Should I care?'

'I'm the father of the boy —' He stopped, began again. 'You threw a stone and broke our window.'

'I did?' The boy sounded politely surprised. 'Can you prove it?'

'You did it, isn't that so? My wife would recognize you.'

'I tell you what,' the dark boy said. 'You got a suspicious mind. You don't want to go around saying things like that – might get you into trouble.'

A fair-haired girl came up, pulled at the tall dark boy's arm. 'Come on, John.'

'Later, Jean. Busy.' He did not stop looking at Brad.

In Brad's stomach the bird was fluttering again, a bird of anger. He said carefully, 'I believe you call the place where I live Snob Hill —'

The boy laughed. 'It's a good name for it.'

'I've come to warn you and your friends to keep away from it. And keep away from my son.'

Fatty crowed in a falsetto voice, 'Don't touch my darling boy.'

'Do I make myself clear?'

'John,' the girl said. 'Don't let's have any trouble. Please.'

The tall dark boy looked Brad up and down. Then smiled. 'We do what we like. It's a free country, they say, and if we want to come up to Snob Hill, see your son, we do it. But I'll tell you what – we'd like to make you happy. If you haven't got the money to pay for the window –' Brad raised a hand in protest, but it was ignored '– we'll have a whip round in The Club here. How's that?'

He laughed, and behind him came the sound of other laughter, sycophantic and foolish. They were all laughing at Brad, and it was hard now to control the bird that leaped inside him. He would have liked to smash the sneering face in front of him with his fist.

But what he did in fact was to run up the steps to the street, get into his car, slam it into gear, and drive hurriedly away. It was as though some fury were pursuing him; but there was no fury, nothing worse than the sound – which he continued to hear in his ears during most of the drive home – of that mocking laughter.

*

When he opened the living-room door their faces were all turned to him – Porky's, Geoff's, Peter's, eager and expectant. He stared at the three of them with a kind of hostility, even though they were his friends. Geoff was their spokesman.

'We were talking again, Brad, about that idea.'

'Idea?' He went over and poured whisky.

'The Residents' Committee. We all think it's pretty good, something we should have done a long while ago. We came to ask if you'd let us nominate you for chairman.'

'Brad!' That was Miriam, who had come in from the kitchen with coffee on a tray. 'Whatever are you doing?'

'What?' Then he realized that he had poured whisky for himself without offering it to his guests. He said, 'Sorry,' and filled their glasses. Porky was watching him with the ironical gaze.

'Hear you bearded the tigers on your own, Brad. How did it go?'

Miriam asked in a high voice, 'Did you see them? Are they going to pay for the window?'

'I saw them. They're louts, hooligans.'

'Of course they are,' Peter fluted.

'I told them some home truths, but it's impossible to talk to them. They —' But he found that he could not go into the humiliating details. 'They've got a kind of club. I saw them there, and I met the ringleader. I shall go to the police tomorrow morning.'

Porky stared at him, but said nothing. Geoff threw up his hands. 'You won't get anywhere with the police.'

Miriam came over to him. 'They *will* do something? Surely we've got a right to protection. We don't have to let them do what they like, do we? They frighten me, Bradley.'

'The best form of protection is self-protection,' Porky said, and expanded on it. 'We've got the nucleus of a Residents' Committee right here. We can easily get another dozen to join us, mount guard at night, look after our own properties. And if we find these tigers, we'll know how to deal with them.'

Miriam looked at Brad inquiringly. It seemed to him that they all waited on his judgement. Just for a moment a picture came into his mind – the picture of a tiger with the dark sneering face of John Baxter, a tiger being hunted through the gardens of The Oasis. Then the picture vanished as though a shutter had been placed over it. What was all this nonsense about tigers?

Brad Fawcett, a liberal with a small 'l', began to speak.

'I think we should be extremely careful about this. I'm not saying it isn't a good idea; I think it is, and I'm inclined to agree that it should have been set up long ago. But I do say we ought to think more carefully about ways and means. There are lots of aspects to it, but essentially it's a community project, and since you've been good enough to come to me, may I suggest that the first step is to sound out our fellow residents and see how many of them like the idea. . .'

As he went on he found that verbalization brought him self-assurance, as it did when he got up to speak as chairman of the Rotary Club. He was not disturbed by the unwinking stare of Porky's little eyes, and if Geoff Cooper looked bored and Peter Stone disappointed, he pretended not to notice it.

They talked for another half hour and drank some more whisky, and by the time the others said good night, see you on the 9:12, the recollection of the visit to Denholm had become no more than a faint disturbance inside him, like indigestion. It did not become urgent again even when Miriam, gripping him tightly in bed, whispered, 'You *will* go to the police in the morning, won't you?'

Sleepily he said that he would – before he caught his train.

At 11:30 the following morning he was preparing with his secretary, Miss Hornsby, an intricate schedule for a conference to begin at noon. The conference was about the installation of new boilers, and his mind was full of maintenance costs when he picked up the telephone.

Miriam's voice asked, 'What did they say?'

For a moment he did not know what she was talking about, so utterly had he shut away that unsatisfactory interview at the police station. Then he remembered.

'The police? They seemed to think we were making a mountain out of a molehill. Perhaps they were right.'

'But what did they *say?*'

'They said if we could identify the boy who broke the window –'

'We can,' she said triumphantly. 'Paul can. He knows them.'

'They explained that it would mean Paul being the chief witness. He would be examined, perhaps cross-examined, in court. We don't want that, do we?'

In her high voice she said, 'I suppose not.'

'Of course we don't. At the moment he's taken it quite calmly. I can't think of anything worse than dragging him through the courts.'

'No.' There was silence. Miss Hornsby raised her eyebrows, pointed at her watch. With the note of hysteria in her voice, Miriam said, 'I'm sorry to bother you —'

'It's all right. I should have phoned you, but I've had a lot of work piled up, still have.'

'Isn't there *anything* the police can do?'

'I've told you what they said.' He was patient; he kept

the irritation out of his voice. 'We'll talk about it later.'

'What time will you be home? Can you come home early?'

Still patiently, speaking as though to a child, he said, 'I have to go into conference at noon, and I don't know when I shall be free. I won't be able to take any phone calls. Pull yourself together, Miriam, and stop worrying.'

As he put down the receiver he saw Miss Hornsby's eyes fixed speculatively on him. He felt guilty, but what had he said that was wrong or untrue? Paul had been tremendously cheerful at breakfast, and had gone off in high spirits. As for the police, the Sergeant had as good as said they had more important crimes to worry about than a broken window. Brad sighed, and returned to the schedule.

He came out of the conference six hours later, feeling tight and tense all over. The client had queried almost everything in the estimate, from the siting of the boilers to the cost of the material used for lining them. He had finally agreed to revise the whole plan. Miss Hornsby had sat in, making notes, but when he got back to his room her assistant, a scared-looking girl, came in.

'Your wife telephoned, Mr Fawcett. Three times. She said it was very important, but you'd said nothing at all must be put through, so —'

'All right. Get her for me.'

'I hope I did right.'

'Just get her for me, will you?'

Half a minute later Miriam's voice, in his ear, was crying, 'They've got him, they've got him, Bradley – he's gone!'

'What are you talking about?'

'Paul. He's not come home from school. He's an hour and a half late.'

'Have you called the school?'

'Oh, yes, yes,' she cried, as though eager to get as quickly as possible through all such silly questions and force on him realization of what had happened. 'I've spoken to them. He left at the usual time. I've been down to the common, he hasn't been there, I've done everything. Don't you see, Bradley, those boys have *taken* him. After you went to see them last night, this is their – their revenge.'

He saw again John Baxter's face, dark and sneering; he remembered the things that had been said in The Club; he knew that the words she spoke were true. Heavily he said, 'Yes. Leave it to me.'

'Bradley, what are they doing to my little boy?'

'He's my boy too,' he said. 'I'll get him back. Leave it to me.'

When he had hung up he sat for a moment, and felt the bird leaping in his belly again. You try to treat them decently, he thought, you try to be reasonable and discuss things with them, and this is what you get. They are like animals, and you have to treat them like animals. He dialled Porky Leighton's number.

Porky wasted no time in saying, 'I told you so.' He was brisk. 'This calls for action, old man. Agreed?'

'Yes.'

'Right, then. This is what we do. . .'

A thin rain was falling as they pulled up outside The Club. They grouped on the pavement, and Brad pointed down the steps. Porky led the way, the others followed. The door was closed, but it opened when Porky turned the handle. There was no sound of music inside and the room seemed to be empty.

'Nobody here,' Geoff Cooper said disgustedly. Then two figures came out from the other end of the room, behind the band platform.

Brad cried out, 'There he is.'

The four of them advanced on the boy. Porky brought him crashing to the floor with a rugger tackle. There was a short scuffle and then, in a moment it seemed, the boy's hands were tied behind his back.

The boy's companion launched herself at Porky. It was the fair-haired girl who had been with Baxter the previous night. Geoff and Peter held her. She was wearing jeans and a boy's shirt.

'Hard to know if it's a boy or girl,' Peter said. He put his hand on her and laughed on a high note. 'You can just about tell.'

The girl cried out, and Porky turned on Peter. 'Cut it out. None of that – you know what we're here for. We've got no quarrel with you, you aren't going to get hurt,' he said to the girl. He spoke to Baxter. 'You know why we're here.'

The boy spoke for the first time. 'You're off your beat, fatso. Shove off.'

They had gone to The Oasis before coming down here, and changed into the old clothes they wore on week-ends for gardening or cleaning the car – clothes so different from their neat daily wear as to be in themselves a kind of uniform. Porky's thick jersey made him look fatter than usual. He was wearing gym shoes, and he balanced himself carefully on his toes.

'Just a few questions, Baxter. Answer them and we won't have any trouble. Where's the gang? Why is the place empty?'

'It's not club night.'

'Why are you here?'

'Cleaning up for tomorrow. What's it to you?'

Porky stuck his red face close to the boy's dark one, jerked a thumb at Brad. 'Know him?'

'That drip. He was in here last night.'

'You know his son. Where is he?'

Baxter looked at him with a half sneer, half smile. 'Tucked up in bed – would that be the right answer?'

Brad saw Porky's hand, large as a knuckle of ham, swing back and slap Baxter's face. The bird leaped inside him, throbbed so violently that his chest was tight. There was a ring on Porky's finger, and it had cut the boy's cheek.

'Not the right answer,' Porky said. 'The boy's been kidnapped. By your friends, while you've fixed yourself a pretty little alibi to keep out of trouble. We want to know where he is.'

'I'll tell you what to do.'

'What?'

Baxter sneered. 'Ask a policeman.'

The bird fluttered up into Brad's throat. He moved toward Baxter with his fist raised. He wanted to speak, but he was breathing so hard he could say nothing intelligible.

After that it was all dreamlike. He participated in what was done – binding up the girl's mouth so that she could not cry out, locking the basement door, bundling the boy out into the car; but it did not seem to him that Bradley Fawcett was doing these things. Another person did them – somebody who had been released from Bradley Fawcett's habitual restraints. In this release there was freedom, some kind of freedom.

They had come in his car, and as he drove back he took a hand from the driving wheel and passed it over his face. He was not surprised to find the skin damp, cold, unfamiliar. He absented himself from the presence of the others in the car, and thought about Miriam – how she had clung to him when he returned, and had begged him to go back to the police.

No, we're going to deal with it ourselves, he had told her quietly and patiently, as he took off his city clothes and put on his week-end ones. Who were 'we'? Porky and the others who had come to the house last night.

'What are you doing to do?'

'See them. Find out what they've done with Paul. Get him back.'

'You really think that's best?' Without waiting for him to say yes, she went on, 'You won't do anything to make them hurt Paul, will you?'

The very thought of Paul being hurt had made him feel sick and angry. 'What do you think I am?' he asked, and as he repeated the words he was aware that they were a question – and one to which he could provide no simple answer, as he could have done a few days or even a few hours earlier.

As he was leaving she had come up and held him close to her. 'It's all our fault, isn't it?'

'*Our* fault?'

'Something to do with us. People like us.'

He had stared at her, then disengaged her arms, and left the house...

They took the boy into the garage. His arms were still tied behind his back. The small cut on his cheek had dried. He made no attempt to call for help, or even to speak, but simply looked at them.

'All right,' Porky said. 'That saw bench over there is just the job, Geoff. Agreed?' He had brought in with him from the car a small leather attache case, and now he took out of it a length of rope. Geoff and Peter bent Baxter over the saw bench.

'Stop,' Bradley Fawcett said. 'What are you doing?'

'He needs a lesson. All agreed on that, aren't we? Let's give him one. Here's teacher.' And now Porky took something else from the attache case and held it up, laughing. It was a thick leather strap.

As the bird inside him fluttered and leaped and hammered on his chest trying to get out, Bradley Fawcett said in a strange voice, 'We must ask him first. Don't do anything without asking him again first.'

Porky's glance at him was amused, contemptuous, tolerant. 'We've asked already, but let's do it according to Hoyle.' Casually he said to Baxter, 'Where's Paul? What have you done with him?'

Baxter spat out an obscenity. 'If I knew, d'you think I'd tell you?' And he spat out another obscenity.

'Very nice.' Porky savoured the response almost with pleasure. 'You see what we're up against, Brad. He's a tiger. We must show him we're tigers too.'

Brad took no part in stretching the boy over the bench and securing his feet. Instead, he considered wonderingly the garage in which everything was stacked tidily–the mower in one corner with its small bag of spanners beside it; the hoe, rake, garden shears, standing in racks; the packets of grass seed and weed-killer on a shelf; Paul's canoe suspended by pulleys. Surely this was the apparatus of a harmless and a decent life?

Yet he knew that he would never again be able to look at these things without thinking of the intrusion among them of this boy with his insolent manner and his strange clothing – the boy who was now bent over the saw bench with his trousers down around his ankles and some of his flesh visible, while Porky stood to the right of him holding the strap and Geoff tucked the boy's head firmly under his arm.

Brad took no part, but he found himself unable to move or to speak while the bird leaped within him, was quiet, then leaped again in its anxiety to escape as the belt descended and a red mark showed on the white flesh. The bird leaped violently at the sight of that red mark and Brad jerked a hand up in the air – but what did he mean to say with that outstretched hand? Was it a gesture of encouragement or of rejection?

He wondered about this afterwards and was never able to know if the answer he gave was honest; but at the time he could not wonder what the gesture meant for the garage door opened, Paul stood framed in it, and Brad was the first to see him. Brad said nothing, but he made a noise in his throat and pointed, and Porky half turned and lowered the strap.

'Dad,' Paul said. 'Mr Leighton. I saw a light. What are you doing?'

In his voice there was nothing but bewilderment. He had his school cap on, he looked handsome and detached, as an adult might look who had discovered children playing some ridiculous secret game.

Bradley Fawcett ran forward, grabbed his son's arm and shook it, trying to shake him out of that awful detachment, and said in a voice which he was horrified to hear come out as high and hysterical as his wife's, 'Where have you been? What's happened to you?'

'Happened? I went to Ainslie's party. Ainslie Evans, you know him.'

'Why didn't you tell anybody? You've got no right —' He could not think what it was that Paul had no right to do.

'But I did tell – I told Mummy yesterday morning. She must have forgotten.'

Paul took his arm away from his father's hand. He was looking beyond Brad to where Geoff and Peter were untying John Baxter, who drew up his trousers. 'Why were you beating John? Have you kidnapped him or something? Is this your idea of a joke?'

Porky gave a short snarl of laughter.

Paul went on. 'It's something to do with that broken window, isn't it?' Now he faced his father and said deliberately, 'I'll tell you something. I'm glad they broke that window.'

'Paul,' Brad cried out. He held out his hand to his son,

but the boy ignored it. Paul stood in the doorway and seemed about to say something decisive, irrevocable. Then the door closed behind him.

John Baxter had his trousers zipped. He looked from one to the other of them. 'It was assault. I could make a case out of it. If I wanted.'

'It was a mistake.' Geoff cleared his throat. 'I don't know about the others, but I don't suppose you'd say no to a fiver.' He took out his wallet.

Peter already had his wallet out.

Porky said, 'Don't be silly.' They stared at him.

'Have you forgotten who he is? He's the little punk who daubs garages and breaks windows. What are you giving him fivers for – to come back and do it again?' When he spoke to John Baxter, the cords of his thick neck showed clearly. 'You were lucky. You just got a little taste of what's good for you. Next time it might be more than a taste, eh, Brad?'

'It's done now,' Brad said mechanically. He was not thinking of the boy, but of the look on Paul's face.

'Don't worry,' Baxter said. 'You can stuff your money. But next time you come our way, look out.'

'We won't — ' Geoff began to say.

'Because next time we'll be ready for you, and we'll cut you. So look out.'

Then the garage door closed behind him too, and Porky was saying with a slight laugh, as he snapped his attache case, 'All's well that ends well, no harm done, but you certainly want to be careful of what your wife says, Brad old man.'

The bird fluttered again within him, and he found relief in shouting, 'Shut up!'

Peter Stone fluted at him. 'I think you're being unreasonable. We were doing it for you.'

'Get out!' Brad held open the door. Outside was darkness

'You're overwrought.' Porky was smiling. 'A good night's sleep's what you need, Brad old man.'

They walked away down the path, Porky with a slight swagger, Peter Stone with an air of being the injured party. Geoff Cooper was last. He gave Brad's arm a slight squeeze and said, 'You're upset. I don't blame you. See you on the 9:12.'

I never want to see you again; you have made me do things I never intended – things I know to be unworthy: those were the words he cried out in his mind, but they remained unspoken.

He stood there for some minutes after the sound of their footsteps faded, and looked at the light in the house which showed that Miriam was waiting to receive him in a gush of apologetic tears; and as he stood there he came slowly to the realization that Porky was right in saying no harm had been done.

A young tough had got a stripe on his backside, and very likely it would do him good. And as for Paul, it was absurd to think that what he had seen would affect him, or their relationship, permanently.

Bradley Fawcett's thoughts drifted away, and suddenly he found that instead of being concerned with Paul he was reliving that moment in which leather struck flesh and the bird had leaped violently, passionately, ecstatically, within him.

As he dismissed these thoughts and walked over to the house and the lighted window, he reflected that of course he would catch the 9:12 in the morning. There was for him, after all, no other train to take.

THE DUPE

There was a good deal of argument about the justice of the verdict when Evelyn Ellis was found guilty but insane. It is not likely, anyway, that she would have been hanged; but, curiously enough, it was the particular person Evelyn chose to kill, and the first words she spoke to the police afterwards, that influenced the jury most strongly in reaching their verdict. And so Evelyn Ellis spent the last fifteen years of her life in Broadmoor, where she sang old-fashioned sentimental songs and developed considerable skill in loom-weaving, turning out a quite remarkable variety of scarves and table runners. It is very likely that, with the exception of the few days to be described in this story, those were the happiest years of her life.

In the forty-five years before she went to Broadmoor Evelyn Ellis had had little cause for singing. Her father died when she was six years old; he had been a partner in a shipping agency, and left to his widow a share in this business which was sufficient to keep her and the children in reasonable comfort. It did so for a few years until Ellis's partner, who had been carrying on the agency single-handed, went abroad in a hurry. He had always been perfectly charming to Mrs Ellis, and the revelation that he had been diverting large sums of money from the agency to his private use profoundly shocked her. She was at first too dazed to appreciate fully the change in her circumstances from prosperity to sharp poverty; when she finally undersood that life held for her no prospect but that of finding some kind of job to keep herself and her two daughters, Mrs Ellis took an overdose of veronal. She left a letter to her sister Lavinia, with whom she had quarrelled bitterly several years before, begging her to provide for the education of Evelyn and Agnes.

Aunt Lavinia did her best for the children after her fashion, which was that of the hard-headed wife of a hard-headed wholesaler in cotton goods. She paid for their education at a shabby-genteel private school, where they learned very little and were rather poorly fed. They stayed at school during most holidays for Aunt Lavinia, who had intensely disliked her woolly-minded sister, had no particular desire to see her sister's children.

It was at school, during holiday time, that the incident occurred which marred Evelyn's whole life. She was fourteen years old and her sister was twelve when Evelyn playfully pushed Agnes, as they stood at the head of the stairs leading to the school library. Agnes slipped, fell down the dozen stairs to the bottom, and lay there laughing at her sister and saying that she could not get up. Agnes had, in fact, fractured her spine. She lay on her back for many months, seen, probed at and discussed by a variety of doctors who were, as Aunt Lavinia told the sisters more than once, a great expense. The months developed into years, and gradually it was understood and accepted by everybody, including Agnes herself, that she would never walk normally again. She was not completely helpless, for with the aid of sticks she was able to walk a few steps to a chair where she half sat, half lay, but anything like a normal life was impossible for her.

Perhaps it seems strange that the effect of the accident was to bind the sisters more closely together. Agnes apparently felt no resentment for the push that had turned her from a healthy, laughing girl into a cripple. Evelyn, on the other hand, felt a burden of guilt about her sister that could never be removed. Her life was dedicated to making Agnes happy. When she took a secretarial job in London Agnes came with her to share the tiny flat in suburban Balham which was all she could afford. Before leaving for work every day Evelyn made her own and Agnes's breakfast, and helped her sister to dress. During the daytime Agnes sat in a chair by their first floor window and watched what went on in the street. She became a well-known figure in the neighbourhood as she waved gaily and called a greeting to children, tradesmen and neighbours. The landlady, Mrs Norton, who cooked midday dinner every day and brought it up to Agnes, was full of admiration for her cheerfulness. 'Your sister is wonderful, Miss Evelyn,' she used to say. 'Always merry and bright.' And indeed Agnes was always smiling and had a beautiful fresh complexion, in contrast to Evelyn whose face was sallow, and wore a perpetually harassed look.

When Evelyn was twenty-eight she met an elderly man named Edward Ryan, who worked in the accounts department of the insurance company in which she was a secretary. Ryan took her out half a dozen times, to theatres and dances, and twice to dinner. On these evenings, of course, Agnes was left alone, although Mrs Norton came up to have a chat with her. Agnes asked her sister quietly whether she had had a nice time, but her high colour was a little higher and her bright eyes a little brighter than usual when Evelyn returned home. On the second occasion when Edward Ryan took Evelyn to dinner, one of the fears about her sister that haunted Evelyn became a reality. In walking, with the aid of sticks, from bed to chair, Agnes had slipped and fallen. She had been badly shaken although she had managed to get back to bed. All this Agnes told Evelyn, her bright eyes fixed with unwavering intensity upon her sister's face. Afterwards Evelyn whispered a guilty 'Yes' to her sister's questions about having a nice time. The next day she told Edward Ryan that she could not go out with him any more, and shortly afterwards she found another job.

In those days Evelyn still had a kind of anxious prettiness of which nothing remained in the gaunt, sallow woman who seventeen years later stood in the dock on a charge of murder. At the time of her trial Evelyn was employed as assistant in Mr Pettigrew's antiquarian bookshop just off Piccadilly. Mr Pettigrew was a second cousin of Aunt Lavinia, who had positively cast off the sisters when Evelyn refused to consider the idea that Agnes would be better off in a nursing home. Mr Pettigrew said that he gave Evelyn a job because he was sorry for her, but he may have kept her on because she typed his letters and kept his books for a smaller salary than he would have had to pay anyone else. She had no specialised knowledge of books, but that was not very important, for she was only left in charge of the shop between four and six o'clock. Just before four o'clock each day, after drinking his cup of afternoon tea, plump, neat little Mr Pettigrew went home. He always made the same joke when he left. 'Remember you are the guardian of my treasures, Miss Ellis,' he said. 'If anybody tries to take them from you, just show them Jessie.' Jessie was the old revolver, tucked away in a drawer at the back of the shop. But not many customers came in between four and six o'clock, and although a few of them were rather odd, there was never any need to show them Jessie.

For that matter, although Mr Pettigrew had some handsome sets of standard authors in finely-tooled bindings, his bookshop did not contain such wonderful treasures as all that – not like the jeweller's next door, with its half dozen clasps, necklaces and single stones discreetly displayed on velvet behind steel-barred windows. Evelyn always lingered to look at the jeweller's window after shutting the shop and saying good night to Williams, the night watchman of the bank on the other side of Pettigrew's, who also included the jeweller's and the bookshop in his nightly round. Williams came on duty a few minutes before Evelyn left at night, and he used often to watch her looking into the jeweller's window. At such times her lips moved, although no sound could be heard – an odd uncomfortable habit which had been noticed by Mr Pettigrew. The little bookseller had also observed that Evelyn had begun to read voraciously the kind of love stories that are generally bought by teenage shop girls. She also appeared at the bookshop one day with some clumsily-applied lipstick on her mouth.

Middle-aged spinsters do tend, however, to odd ideas and habits, as plump Mr Pettigrew commented to his wife, and there was nothing wrong with Evelyn's work. Probably she would have gone on working for Mr Pettigrew and looking after Agnes until the end of her life, if it had not been for Millie Hanslet, who took a room on the ground floor of the house in Balham. Millie Hanslet was a brass-haired, loud-voiced, fiftyish woman who said that she lived on a small annuity and a widow's pension for her husband, who had been killed in Africa during the war. Millie came up sometimes in the evening to have a cup of tea with the Ellises, and to bemoan quite frankly the absence of men in her life. 'A woman needs a man,' she said. 'I mean someone to go about with, take her to the pictures, buy ice cream. Isn't that so?'

'I don't know,' said Agnes coldly, from her chair by the window.

Millie Hanslet gave a great wink at Evelyn, who smiled back at her uncertainly. 'And *I'm* going to get a man,' she added. 'You see.'

When Millie had gone downstairs Agnes said: 'She's vulgar.'

'Yes, I suppose so,' Evelyn sighed. Then she began to get supper.

Four days later Millie Hanslet came upstairs and produced triumphantly a small snap of a flashily handsome young man with a moustache. 'That's my beau.'

Agnes hardly looked at it. Evelyn asked excitedly, 'How did you meet him?'

'Pen Friends Unlimited,' Millie said triumphantly. Evelyn merely looked mystified. Millie explained: 'It's only a couple of pounds to join, and then they give you the names of half a dozen gentlemen and give them *your* name, and you write to each other and exchange photographs, and if you want to meet each other you do. Here's the leaflet.' Evelyn took it automatically. Her eyes were still on the photograph in Millie's hand.

Later that evening Agnes said: 'My back hurts. I think I'll go to bed now.' Evelyn helped her sister into bed. Agnes's face, round and almost youthful by the side of Evelyn's, was anxious. 'You're not going to write to those pen-friend people, are you?'

'Of course not,' Evelyn said, and hoped that she sounded convincing. She wrote next day, using the address of Pettigrew's Bookshop. There was no danger of Mr Pettigrew's seeing the reply, because Evelyn was always there first to open the post. When writing, Evelyn took eight years off her age, calling herself thirty-seven. She described herself as fair-haired and vivacious, said that she was fond of good books, good music and the theatre, and wanted to correspond with a gentleman under forty who had similar interests. She received a reply by return post, which she opened with trembling fingers. It was a short letter which thanked her for her postal order, and said that her name had been put on the register of Pen Friends Unlimited. She would realise that most gentlemen under forty were interested in meeting ladies younger than themselves, but her name had been passed to two or three possible pen friends who might be interested.

Two days later the letter came. It began 'Dear Pen-Friend Evelyn' and was signed 'Yours very sincerely, Colin (Jameson).'

The writer of the letter said that he was thirty-three years old, and liked the older and more sensible type of woman. 'These modern flappers with their painted faces and painted toe-nails drive me to distraction,' the letter said. 'I don't want the woman of my choice to be a frump, but I do want her to have some ideas beyond paint and powder.' He enclosed a photograph which showed a rather ruggedly determined-looking man with thick eye-brows and dark hair growing low over his forehead. He did not look much more than thirty years old.

Evelyn read the letter a dozen times. She had a number of photographs taken in her only recent frock, and selected one from them which, if looked at with a friendly eye, made her seem no more than forty. She was hardly prepared, however, for the enthusiasm with which he received it. 'I loved your innocent look,' he wrote in a firm upright hand she looked for now every day in the post. 'And the beautiful spirit that shows in the features. But you must have deceived me about your age. I believe you are younger than I am.' The correspondence flourished. Colin ('You must call me Colin and I shall call you Evelyn,' he wrote in his second letter) worked as a foreman in a large engineering works in North London, on night shift from seven o'clock in the evening until three a.m. He had been left an orphan at the age of eleven – rather like her-self, Evelyn thought – and had then been brought up by a foster-mother. He had worked since he was fourteen. 'I have to admit that I'm not really an educated man,' he wrote, and she loved his frankness. He had married when he was twenty-two, but after three years of unhappy bickering had discovered his wife's unfaithfulness, and divorced her. 'It was foolish of me, dear Evelyn, but this experience turned me against all women for a time. Can you understand that? I think you can, for I believe you have a great knowledge of human nature.' He told her that her letters meant a great deal in the life of a lonely man.

The effect of this correspondence on Evelyn was remarkable. A spirit and gaiety came back into her face that had not been there for years. At the bookshop Mr Pettigrew commented on her cheerfulness, and at home Agnes looked at her with an enquiring eye, although she said nothing. When, however, Millie Hanslet asked if Evelyn had written to Pen Friends Unlimited she received a curt negative answer.

Evelyn Ellis was bemused by the correspondence, but there remained one small shadow of doubt in the fiery dreams of happiness that occupied her every day. It seemed that with Colin working on night shift all the time they would never meet, and sometimes she feared that he must be unreal, or that some old, old man was playing a cruel joke on her. When Colin wrote that he longed for a meeting, she still felt some doubt of him, for he added that on Saturday and Sunday he always went down to see his foster-mother who was bedridden and lived at an Old People's Home near Dorking. 'The old lady hasn't much longer in this world,' he wrote, 'and you wouldn't want me to neglect her.' Evelyn was not suspicious, but she couldn't help feeling that there was something odd about the fact that they could never meet, and when she daringly suggested that he should come to the bookshop one day after Mr Pettigrew had gone home she half-expected to get a letter the next morning with an elaborate excuse for his absence.

But he came. The door opened and he stood there, dark, square and robust, his eyes looking quickly round the shop and then settling on her, his mouth smiling.

Nobody else was in the shop. She ran forward to him.

'You've come.'

'Did you think I wouldn't?' His voice was deep, and in anyone else it might have appeared to her rather common. 'I'd have known you anywhere,' he said, and added quickly, 'We can't talk here. What about coming out to tea?'

She fairly gaped at him. 'But I've told you – you know I can't. . .'

'Why not? What the eye doesn't see the heart doesn't grieve over, as they say. You told me yourself not many people come in after four.'

She hesitated, but only for a moment. Relief at finding that he really existed, that Fate had not played a cruel trick on her, swamped all other feelings. They went to a little teashop that he knew and Evelyn talked as she had not talked for years. She told him about her childhood and the family misfortunes, and for the first time mentioned her sister vaguely, without saying that she was an invalid. Colin did not say very much, but he was a good listener, and occasionally he squeezed her hand. All too soon he looked at his watch and said that he must go to work. He held her hands at parting.

'You'll be here tomorrow?'

'I can't,' she said weakly. 'I oughtn't to shut the shop.'

He dropped her hands.'I thought you were sincere about wanting to see me, but perhaps you just don't care.'

'Oh, I do, I do.'

'Well then if you want to see me like I want to see you. . .'

'All right,' Evelyn said. She felt faint with joy at his eagerness, she would have agreeed to anything. 'I'll be here.'

His face lit up, he smiled charmingly. 'That's my girl. Just after four tomorrow.' In the public street he kissed her goodbye.

That night Agnes guessed the truth that Evelyn, in her happiness, hardly attempted to hide. 'You've met a man.' Evelyn, humming a tune under her breath, said nothing. 'Is it through that beastly Pen Club?

'And if it is?'

'Then he's up to no good. There's something he wants from you.'

Evelyn laughed and turned round. 'Do you think he's after me for my money or my looks?' she asked, but there was no bitterness in her voice. Then the flood of her happiness spilled over. 'Oh Agnes, he's so handsome, so attractive. Not quite – not quite our sort, you know, but what does that matter?'

Agnes stared incredulously at the photograph so proudly displayed by her sister. 'He must be years younger than you are. In some way or other he's fooling you, he's duping you.'

'What way?

Agnes shook her head. 'I don't know, but there's something. You're a dupe, Evie, a dupe. In some way he's using you for a purpose of his own.'

'Agnes! It's just that he likes me. He needn't have met me unless he'd wanted to. He's very lonely, he wants company. . .'

'Does he want it enough to put up with the two of us?' Agnes's voice was high. 'Have you told him about me? Or are you just going to leave me to – look after myself?'

The light in Evelyn's face faded. 'You know I should never do that.'

'And does *he* know it? Have you told him you've got a crippled sister dependent on you?' Agnes's smooth face was almost ugly as she said 'You'd see that would soon make him change his tune about marriage.'

'For heaven's sake, Agnes, there's no question of marriage. Why I only met him today for the first time.'

'You just tell him about your sister, that's all.'

Evelyn and Colin met the next day, and the next, but they did not speak of Agnes. The hands of the watch crawled round each day until they reached four o'clock, Mr Pettigrew made his little joke about his treasures and Jessie, and within five minutes of his departure she was running – yes, positively running – to the teashop where they met, without sparing so much as a glance for the jeweller's next door. He was always there, waiting for her – one day when she was five minutes late he looked quite anxious – and he always made some comment on her appearance, and told her how much her friendship meant to him. They talked, or she talked and he listened, and at quarter-past six each day he left her to go off to work. He was not a gentleman, there could be no doubt of that, but then he made no pretence to be one, and that, she felt, counted in his favour. On Wednesday she said to him, 'I have my half-day off tomorrow.'

He looked quite startled. 'Do you?'

She said shyly, 'I could meet you early – at one o'clock – if you'd like to.'

'Well, I don't know. I never knew you had a half-day off on Thursday.' He said this almost in a tone of annoyance. There was a pause. Then came the sudden smile that charmed her, and he said, 'We'll go to Richmond. What about that?' And at Richmond on the river next day Colin told her again that he was a lonely man and asked if she would consider marriage.

'Oh, Colin.' They kissed. Then she remembered. She must tell him about Agnes. It would be a kind of test, she told herself with a sinking heart; it would show whether his feeling for her was sincere. 'I've got something to tell you. I want you to look away while I'm saying it.'

He took her hands. Beneath the thick brows his eyes were wary. 'Here, here, what's all this about?'

'Look away from me.' He looked into the water, trailing one hand in it, while she told him the story of her sister, confessed the guilt she had always felt, told him of the terrible dream she had had night after night for years in which Agnes, calm and smiling, floated rather than fell down an endless flight of steps with her dress ballooning out like a parachute, and then lay crumpled like a spider at the bottom. All the while he listened with his face turned away as she had asked, his hand trailing in the water. At the end she said, 'So you see I could never leave her,' and knew it was a lie, knew that if he asked her to do it she would leave Agnes and go with him.

But he did not ask her. He took his hand out of the water and smiled at her.

'Is that all? I thought you had something terrible to tell me.'

'You mean it's all right? Agnes can come and live with us?'

'Of course. You don't suppose I'd turn your sister away.'

'Oh Colin!' Words were inadequate to express what she felt. It was as though she was living within a beautiful rose-coloured bubble where everything that she wished for came true. She told Agnes, who was pleased but still suspicious. 'You must bring him round to see me,' she said, and Evelyn promised exultantly that she would. She went downstairs to share her happiness with Millie Hanslet, but Millie Hanslet, Mrs Norton said, had been called away suddenly to her sick mother in Birmingham and had taken all her possessions with her.

That was Thursday. On Friday and Saturday she

saw him again, and on the following Monday the inevitable happened. A customer who had come round at five o'clock on Saturday and found the shop closed had telephoned to Mr Pettigrew about it. Evelyn made stumbling, confused excuses about her sister, and Mr Pettigrew said sharply that this must not happen again, or else. Or else what he did not say, but Evelyn could imagine.

That day she did not go to meet Colin, and at half past four he came to the shop. A customer was there and Colin glowered at the books until the man had gone. Then he turned on her, and she felt the blast of his anger, withering her precious happiness. She appealed to him. What would happen if she lost her job? He snarled at her then – really there was no other word for it – that he had already promised to look after her and her precious sister. What more did she want? Then his tone changed suddenly and he talked to her gently, earnestly, persuasively. There was no other time at which they could meet, he said. Didn't she want to see him, as much as he wanted to see her? His dark head was very close to hers, his lips whispered the reassuring words she had always wanted to hear.

Evelyn met him on Tuesday, and again on Wednesday, when she took him home to meet Agnes. Evelyn had made scones and a jam sponge in advance, and she was a little distressed because Colin did not eat very much. She and Agnes made most of the conversation. Colin was pleasant enough, but he seemed to find the occasion a strain.

'Did you like Agnes?' she asked when she was seeing him on to the bus.

'Eh? Yes, she's all right. Bad luck for her, being an invalid like that.'

'You won't mind living with her?'

'No,' he said as if with an effort. 'No, I shan't mind.'

'Tomorrow's my half-day.'

Again he seemed to be making an effort. 'So it is. What would you like to do, eh?'

'You'll think I'm foolish, but I've never seen the Tower of London.'

'Tower of London?' He stared at her incredulously. 'I thought only kids went there.'

Something in his manner upset her, and she almost gabbled. 'Oh, we won't go if you don't want to, of course, we'll do anything you like, perhaps it's foolish, it was just that I hadn't seen it. . .'

'Here, here.' He stopped her with a laugh. 'Of course we can go there if you want to. I was just a bit surprised, that's all.'

Evelyn was almost in tears. 'But you said only kids. . .'

'Now then,' he said. 'Don't pick me up on everything I say. You're begining to think you're the wife already.'

The bus came. He kissed her, looked at her for a fraction of a second longer than usual, and then jumped on it quickly.

When Evelyn got home she asked eagerly 'Did you like him?'

Agnes said hesitantly, 'I think you ought to be careful, Evie. You don't know anything about him really, do you?'

'I know he's in love with me.' Agnes remained silent. Evelyn's voice had a hysterical note in it. 'He loves me enough to be prepared to live with you. What more do you want?'

'Nothing, Evie,' her sister answered with quite unaccustomed meekness. 'I want you to be happy.'

*

The first blow fell on Thursday morning. Mr Pettigrew reached the shop early for once, and confronted her with an expression of extraordinary grimness. Evelyn had been unlucky. The persistent man who had paid a visit before when the shop was shut had come three times between half-past four and six on Wedneday afternoon. Evelyn had no chance to invent a story, even if she had been capable of it. Mr Pettigrew spoke of vipers in his bosom, of deceit and idleness and the modern worker. She was to leave at the end of the week.

The second blow fell at lunch-time. She was to meet Colin at one o'clock at their teashop, and it was half-past before Evelyn began to understand that he might not be coming. She stayed in the teashop until two o'clock and then wandered out, looking so pale that the woman in charge of it asked if she would like some brandy. All sorts of wild thoughts moved through her mind. Perhaps they had agreed to meet at the Tower itself, perhaps he had been called suddenly to do a daytime shift, perhaps he was ill or hurt. Never for a moment did she admit that he might have broken their appointment deliberately.

At last she took a bus to Holloway and found 133 Bossom Street, the address from which he had written the letters that she cherished. It was a small tobacconist's shop, an accommodation address for receiving letters, and they had not seen Mr Jameson for the past two or three days. At half-past five Evelyn returned to the flat in Balham, hoping that there might be news of him. There was none. Agnes tried to comfort her. 'We still have each other,' she said. Evelyn shuddered.

When Evelyn left on Friday morning to go to work she met the postman and asked, without hope, if there were any letters for her. There *was* a letter, in the familiar firm, upright hand. Her heart leapt. She tore the letter open on the bus with eager, fumbling fingers, and while she read the words seemed to jump before her eyes. The letter said they could not meet again for reasons which she would soon understand, and that she should not take the affair too much to heart. The letter ended, 'I am very sorry it has to be this way, but when I saw you with your sister I realized that your place is really with her and that, even if the right man turns up, you could never marry and leave her. *I hope you can forget that you ever saw me.*' It was signed simply 'Colin'.

At the bookshop a grave Mr Pettigrew awaited her, and with him a lean, kindly man named Inspector Ballard. Evelyn felt like someone walking through a thick mist as the Inspector explained that last night the jeweller's shop next door had been robbed and sixty thousand pounds' worth of stones stolen, and that the night watchman had been stunned and gagged.

Nor did she understand in the least what was being implied when the Inspector told her of the ingenious method employed, of how, down in the basement, sufficient of the brickwork in the wall separating the bookseller's storeroom from the disused basement below the jeweller's shop had been removed to allow the thieves to go through, and how they had avoided the jeweller's burglar alarm system by knocking away the basement ceiling, cutting through the floorboards and going through into the shop upstairs.

It was a neat job, the Inspector said almost admiringly, and of course it needed some sort of co-operation. Or deception, he added with his kindly gaze on Evelyn, or deception. Because it took a good many hours' work to go through that wall, and they wouldn't have dared do it while she was above them because she would have heard, and they couldn't have done it at night because of the watchman making his rounds. It seemed a fair puzzle, the Inspector said, until they discovered from one of the jeweller's assistants that Mr Pettigrew's shop had been shut from four o'clock onwards during the last few days. A few minutes after four a van had been noticed on at least two occasions drawing up, two men had got out with armfuls of books, opened the door of Mr Pettigrew's shop and gone in. The books were a blind, of course, although they would have been useful in case of questioning. The men had put in a couple of hours' work on the basement brickwork and then left before the night watchman came on duty, no doubt roughly replacing the brickwork and covering it with a screen of books. It was simple, the Inspector said, when you knew how.

All this time Evelyn said nothing, but simply twisted her hands together around the bag that contained the letter in the firm upright handwriting. When the Inspector put his questions about where she had been on those days, gently at first, then sharply and finally with downright anger, she simply said that she had gone out each day, she did not know where.

It is doubtful, indeed, if any of his questions touched the simple conviction occupying her mind, that she must keep faith with the man who had shown her a glimpse of what life might be like, and had then left her because he thought her place was really with Agnes. She did not flinch when he showed her the book of photographs, turning the pages slowly and telling her something of the villainous history of this man or that one before asking if she had ever seen them. Not by a flicker of one of her red-rimmed eyelids did she show recognition when he turned to a photograph that showed Colin and Millie Hanslet together and explained that this one's real name was James Johnson, that he called himself Jones or Johns or James or Jameson, that he had been imprisoned more than once for running, with the help of the woman, friendship clubs that were a cloak for blackmail, and that he was often used as a contact man by crooks more important than himself. She remembered the last words of the letter, *I hope you can forget that you ever saw me,* and she let the Inspector turn the page.

When the Inspector at last abandoned his questioning for the time being, in desperation at his inability to break down the barrier of her indifference or ignorance, Evelyn Ellis knew what she must do to preserve her soul alive, as she put it at the trial. She went to the back of the shop to wash her hands, she slipped Jessie out of the drawer into her handbag, she said goodbye calmly to Mr Pettigrew, and then she went home and shot her sleeping sister Agnes through the head. When the police came, Evelyn Ellis made a statement, simple and to her quite satisfactory. 'I had to do it, you see,' she said. 'While she was alive I could never get married.'

Somebody Else

As the years passed it seemed to Melly that the party at the Estersons had been the turning point of her life. In a literal sense this was true, because she met her husband Frederick for the first time on the night of the party; but there was more to it than that. The Estersons' party was crucial because of what happened there, the thing about which she never afterward said anything to anybody, not even to Frederick. And then again, as time went by, she had flickerings of doubt about whether anything had happened at all. Everything, in any case, seemed to depend on the party.

It was a time when she was young and silly, or perhaps when she was recovering from the effects of being young and silly. Her mother had died when she was three years old, and she had been brought up in Singapore by her father. It was true that he sent her to school in England but she made few friends, and the months of each year spent in England seemed to her tedious spaces between the events of her real life.

This life began again with each holiday when she flew back to Singapore and met her father at the airport, a tall, distinctive, immediately recognizable figure, with his Panama hat and ebony walking stick. She knew that he was proud of her from the way in which he introduced her with imperturbable sweet gravity to strangers at parties.

'This is my daughter Melisande,' he would say. 'She was named after my favourite opera.' When she was small he would sometimes read to her a poem about Melisande, a poem that began:

Pale little princess, passionate and shy,
With delicate small hands and heavy hair,
A simple child-like creature, wild and fair,
Yet shadowed by a haunting mystery.

The poem seemed to her very beautiful, and she always called herself by her full name, refusing to speak to the girls at school who abbreviated it. Really, as she afterwards realized, she saw her father very little, for even when she was at home he was in his office all day, often came home late at night, and sometimes did not return that day at all.

So she was alone a great deal, and although she was not conscious of being lonely it was, as he said, no life for a young girl. When she was nineteen she went off (I was *sent* off, she thought later) to a secretarial job in England. He consoled her when she wept, reciting two more lines from that sad poem, lines about her Pelleas entering at the door.

'You don't want to spend your time with an old fellow,' he said. 'In England your Pelleas will be waiting for you.'

He gave her the boyish smile that made the words about being an old fellow quite ridiculous. It was only later, again, remembering the servants giggling together and recalling things hinted by acquaintances, that she realized he had carried on frequent affairs and that the presence of a young daughter must have been an embarrassment. Only later too she understood the meaning of a scene she had witnessed when she was ten years old.

She had come home early from the local school because she felt unwell, to hear a murmur of voices and laughter. One of the voices sounded like her father's, although there was an unusual note in it. The voices came from the living room and, delighted to find him at home, she opened the door. Her first impression was that he was playing a game with a child on the floor. Then she saw that the child was a Chinese girl and that she wore no clothes.

The Chinese girl stared straight at Melisande with no expression at all. Melly could not see her father's face, and retained an impression only of a crouching powerful animal with huge hands that moved up the little Chinese girl's arms to grip her shoulders and, as it seemed, to shake her. Then Melly closed the door and ran to her room.

That was one of the nights on which her father stayed away. The next day he picked her up at school and took her out for a picnic. He never referred to the incident and she did not see the Chinese girl again. A few months later Melly was sent to boarding school in England.

She got the secretarial job through a letter written by her father to a director in a publishing firm, whom he had known long ago when they were undergraduates. Very soon she met a young man who might, she thought, be Pelleas. His name was Archie and he was a commercial artist, but he was suitably ethereal and elegant. He took her out to dinner and to concerts, and kissed her in taxis. She did not greatly enjoy the kissing, and although she permitted him to seduce her in his flat one night because he seemed to expect it, she found that also not particularly enjoyable. He did not say, 'I love you,' and what happened seemed very unromantic and unlike the ideal relationship between Pelleas and Melisande.

The affair with Archie, if it could be called an affair, ended abruptly a few days later when she received a cable saying that her father had died suddenly of a heart attack. She flew back to Singapore for the funeral, and there learned that he had died in bed with his latest mistress, and that he had left nothing but debts. Behind the sympathy of friends she detected a kind of malicious satisfaction. She returned to England as soon as possible. For some reason she had a horror of seeing Archie again, and refused to speak to him when he telephoned.

In the weeks that followed she took a great many pills of various kinds, some on the instructions of her doctor, pills to tranquillize and to enliven, and she mixed these pills with drink so that she was in what seemed a state of continual light-headedness. She worked for Mr Radcliffe, the editorial director who had known her father, and he was very gentle; but he was also ponderously dignified and somehow she was put off by the rimless glasses he wore and the sniffs that punctuated his remarks. When he asked her out to dinner one night, the sniff was distressingly in evidence as he pondered what to order. Then she was irritated when he consulted her about the wine. Her father would never have consulted any lady about the wine.

'The truth is I feel a little responsible for you, my dear. After all, I did know Charles. A remarkable man. He was the leader among our little group at the University, you know. I always thought —'

Mr Radcliffe did not complete the sentence and she did not ask him to do so because it seemed to imply that her father had promised more than he had performed in life, and if that was his opinion she did not want to hear it. 'But in the last few weeks you've been obviously – well, not yourself.' He sniffed.

She sipped the wine. 'Does that mean you want to get rid of me?'

'Not at all. It's just that – well, you've suffered a great tragedy. I think it has affected you.'

'It's true I'm not myself,' she admitted. There was consolation in uttering the words aloud. To be 'not yourself', what did that mean? Did it mean that you were somebody else?

'I should like you to feel that you could come to me with any problems.' Sniff. 'If it would help you to have a few days off, that could easily be arranged.'

'I'm perfectly all right. But thank you, Mr Radcliffe.'

I do believe, she thought, that he's making approaches to me, a man old enough to be – she did not complete the sentence even in her mind. But perhaps she was wrong, for although Mr Radcliffe drove her back to the apartment she shared with another girl he did not even put his hand on her knee, and he refused her invitation to come up for a nightcap. On the following day he was his usual ponderous self and it seemed impossible that he had ever suggested she should call him Donald.

Mr Radcliffe was a bore, there was no denying it, and to her surprise most of the authors she met in the office were boring too. Although some of them wrote about young people they were almost all of them well over forty, and in spite of the fact that, as she gathered with astonishment, few of them made a living from their books, they were tremendously puffed up with their own importance. Some of them tried to flirt with her – it was the only word she could use – and one flirter took her out to lunch and talked about his own books all the time.

Gabriel Esterson was interesting because he was so unlike the other authors. He was tall and fair, with bright blue eyes, a lick of hair that came down over his forehead and an enthusiastic manner. He wore turtleneck shirts, or close-fitting suits with high rolled lapels. He wrote what she supposed were science fiction stories – about subjects like the last man left alive after an atomic war and the way in which he repopulated the world by constructing a machine able to bear children, a procedure worked out in much technical detail. During the course of the story the machines learned how to reproduce with each other and at the end they killed the last man.

One day Esterson stopped in her small office after having seen Mr Radcliffe and asked if she liked the book.

'It was interesting.'

'You didn't like it? Why not say so?'

He sat on the edge of her desk. This was one of his turtleneck days.

'All right, I didn't like it.'

'No need to be uptight about it. What's your name?' She told him and he turned down the corners of his wide mouth. 'Ever have fantastic fun?'

'I don't know what you mean.'

'I don't either, baby.' The door of Mr Radcliffe's room opened. He stood there frowning behind the rimless glasses. Gabriel got off the desk and raised a hand. 'See you.'

'That young man is *not* a very desirable character,' Mr Radcliffe said later.

'How do you mean?'

'To my mind there is something unwholesome about his books. Although of course he is a clever writer, which is why we publish him. I may be old-fashioned.' A sniff. She offered no contradiction. 'He has a strange wife. Her name is Innes. I shouldn't be surprised if she takes drugs, she is like a skeleton.'

'Oh.'

'And then they give very odd parties.'

'You've been to them?'

'To one only. We wore masks painted to represent politicians and animals.'

She echoed stupidly, 'Politicians and animals.'

'They fought together. Or pretended to fight. It was all something to do with the release of energy, according to Esterson. I found it distasteful.'

Distasteful, or fantastic fun? A week later Esterson telephoned and asked her to a party on the following Saturday. 'Bring a boy friend if you want to, but I'd like to know now. The number of guests is important.'

'I'll be alone.' She had had no boy friend since Archie.

'Fantastic.'

'Is there something special —'

'Baby, about my parties there's always something special. Not before nine o'clock, not after ten. After ten the gates are locked, we shut the prisoners in. And wear old clothes. Don't dress up, dress down.'

His laugh was infectiously gay. She looked forward to the party. He was not exactly her image of Pelleas and in any case he was married, but there was something exciting about the whole prospect. And maybe she would meet Pelleas at the party.

On Thursday she got the flu. She stayed in bed and Olivia, the girl with whom she shared the apartment, telephoned Mr Radcliffe. During the day she took a variety of pills and felt better, but in the evening she was running a temperature.

On Friday morning she was a little better again, and then in the evening felt really ill. Olivia was going away to her parents for the weekend. She wanted to call a doctor. Melisande told her not to be ridiculous.

'But, Melly —'

'My name is Melisande.'

'You're just being stupid.'

'I'm going to this party tomorrow night, remember.'

'You must be crazy.'

Melisande had difficulty getting Olivia into focus. Sometimes she wavered about as though under water and at other times she was quite distinct, but there were two of her. Olivia took off her clothes preparatory to changing her dress and stood, naked but for brassiere and briefs, in the middle of the room. Melisande looked away for some reason. Olivia was a rather flat-faced girl with dark eyes, and for a moment Melisande had the impression she was looking at the Chinese girl in Singapore.

'You —' She sat up in bed.

'Yes?'

'Nothing. You are Olivia?'

'Look here, I think you're delirious.'

'No, I was just being stupid. You said so, remember? I'm perfectly all right.'

She watched to see if Olivia changed again while she dressed, but nothing happened. When she rushed off finally to catch her train after dithering about making fresh lemon juice, Melisande felt nothing but relief. She took four of her pills and fell asleep almost immediately.

When she woke, light was filtering through the thin curtains. Her vision was clear, her mind vacant, and she stared for what seemed to be minutes at the pattern of wild flowers on the wallpaper, and then she put out her fingers to touch them. The wall was tangibly there but that created a problem for it meant that she was at home, really at home again in Singapore.

Turning over and closing her eyes she saw again and more vividly the wild flowers on the wallpaper, a pattern which her father had ordered because he said she looked like a wild flower herself. Columbine, eglantine, larkspur, what were the names? The larkspur was a brilliant blue. In a moment she would hear the padding feet of the servants or her father singing an old song as he always did before taking his bath:

Don't go walking down Lover's Lane

With somebody else. . .

He always said 'somebody else' instead of the correct words, 'anyone else.' Who was somebody else? She opened her eyes and looked at the clock, which said ten minutes past four. How could it say that when daylight was showing through the curtains? She turned over again and looked at the wall which was now a neutral biscuit colour, devoid of any kind of flower. She was in her rather dingy bedroom in the apartment.

'Afternoon,' she said. 'I've slept for twenty-four hours.'

It was not twenty-four but she could not be bothered to work out the exact number. She got out of bed, went to the lavatory, drank a glass of water, and tried without success to find her pulse. She stuck a thermometer into her mouth and took it out when she felt her eyes closing. The reading seemed to be 102. Utterly weary, she crawled back into bed again and closed her eyes.

She opened them a moment later and looked at the clock, which now said eight fifteen. She remembered the party, got out of bed, and decided that she felt much better. The thermometer lay on the bathroom shelf but she did not use it. Instead she ran a very hot bath, put in double the amount of bath oil she generally used, and immersed herself for twenty minutes. Later she rubbed the steam from the mirror and considered her face and body.

Pale little princess, passionate and shy – but in fact she was a biggish girl, with bones that distinctly stuck out, long twine-coloured hair, a face with neat ears and bright eyes but rather too long a nose, breasts of no particular importance, a good flat stomach, and reasonably attractive legs. It was unremarkable physical equipment for a princess, but would Pelleas think so?

An hour later, after eating with difficulty a tunafish sandwich and taking two pep pills, she was on her way to the party. She was lucky enough to find a taxi just at the door.

There is an area lying between St John's Wood and Maida Vale where the streets are wide, the houses large and Victorianly solid, and the pervading air is one of decayed gentility which has not yet changed to smartness. The

Estersons lived in one of these houses.

Gabriel came to the door, took both her hands in his, then decided to kiss her.

'Baby, you're here. Fantastic. This is Innes. My wife, Melisande.'

'Melisande.' Her name was repeated faintly, with a dying fall. Innes Esterson was tall and extremely thin, with a long white face and drooping shoulders. She wore a bright green shirt and tight-fitting trousers. She peered through short-sighted eyes and murmured again, 'Melisande.' Then she added, 'Your clothes.'

Melly had not quite known how to take Gabriel's instructions and was wearing a blue dress which although not fashionable hardly came in the category of old clothes.

'Perfectly all right,' Gabriel said. 'Super. Come and meet people.'

Twenty of them were standing in a large high-ceilinged living room. Most of the men and some of the women wore pullovers and narrow trousers, but she was glad to see some other dresses. She found a drink in her hand, sipped it, discovered that it had a pleasant bitter-sweetness like some dimly remembered medicine, and drank it down. The glass was refilled almost at once.

She sat on a sofa with a young man who wore long side-burns and talked about underground films. Names slipped off his tongue – Grabowski, Smith, Flugheimer. She caught hold of one and repeated it faintly. 'Masters?'

'Bud Masters. That's me.'

'You're an – underground film maker.' She had a vision of him living underground. He made films there, working in large windowless rooms like boxes. Men and women moved around in them, oscillating slowly and never speaking. At his word of command, 'Action,' they speeded up and began to jerk, never straying from their set positions while he moved among them with his hand-held camera going snap, snap. Later in the dark room, in the darkest of the windowless boxes, he developed the films which showed – what did they show?

'Does underground film making take place underground?' This reasonable question was answered with a laugh. Then Bud Masters vanished and a woman with short-cut hair and a thin nose, wearing a monocle, sat next to her.

'Darling, you're a wit.'

'Who are you?'

'I'm Lenya. What do you do?'

At that moment she could not remember, and so repeated the question. Lenya laughed and her monocle dropped. She replaced it.

'I'm on the box.'

On the box? 'The underground box?' Melly ventured. 'No windows?'

Lenya laughed again. This time the monocle stayed in. 'The idiot box, darling, the hot cod's eye, on your nelly, the telly. Down Our Street – it's been my bread and butter for six months. But they're killing me next week.'

'I'm sorry.'

Lenya leaned toward her and their shoulders touched. 'What's the idea tonight, what's Gabriel up to?' Melly shook her head and sipped her drink. 'I mean, he's always up to something. He's a fun man, isn't he? Were you at the Lies and Truth party?'

'No.'

'We all wore masks and had to tell lies about our past lives. Of course they were almost all about sex. Then there was a psychologist here who analyzed the stories. To Gabriel it was a kind of game – everything's a game to him.'

'And Innes?'

'Innes of course is – well, I mean, she's Innes. But Gabriel, he's never grown up.'

Melisande withdrew her shoulder from the warmth of contact. Gabriel was standing over them, with two men beside him.

'Get up, Lenya, this is round one, and clinches are not allowed until round five.' He took Lenya by the hand and raised her to her feet.

'You know what you are, Gabriel, you're just a damn creep,' she said without heat.

'Better men than you have said worse. You can't monopolize the loveliest girl in the room. Upsadaisy.' His hand, which felt very cool, took Melisande's and she was standing up. Her body felt weightless. He introduced her to the two men, but she did not hear their names. One was an artist and the other a public relations man connected with an American film company.

She listened to them, but although she heard what they said it did not quite seem to make sense. Even the words they used were unfamiliar. Psychedelic she had heard often, although she was never quite sure what it meant; but what was 'a hard-edge painting'? And what was 'kinetic art'? She began to drift, or float, away from them but was hauled back by a question.

'Is this your thing?' It was the artist, plump and red-cheeked. 'I mean, Gabriel's kind of thing, does it turn you on?'

'I don't know,' she said truthfully. 'What kind of thing is it?'

'That's the question.' The artist looked at the public relations man. 'Isn't that the question, Bruno?'

'You're right there, Whit. With Gabriel that's always the question.' Bruno had a bristly moustache and bulging eyes. 'Shall I tell you something? I fancy you.'

If I had some vanishing cream, she thought, I could smear it on that nasty little moustache and it would disappear. And if I had *enough* vanishing cream I could smear it all over him and then *he* would disappear. The idea made her giggle.

'What's so funny?' asked Bruno Moustache, but without answering this she did drift or float away to find herself talking to Innes, who spoke in a faint expiring voice, in gasps like a swimmer pushing a head up out of water and then dropping back. For some reason they were talking about the nature of experience.

'You don't think then – that there's anything in – mysticism? In getting – beyond the self?'

Melly considered this. 'I don't know. I've never had an experience like that.'

'Gabriel believes that what Western man feels – is limited by his – environment.' Innes' eyes were little colourless pills set in deep sockets alongside her long nose. 'He thinks we should try to – reach out – to something beyond – ourselves.'

The words seemed to sound an echo in her mind. 'Yes.'

'That's what his work is – all about.' Innes raised an arm almost as thin as a clothesline and let it drop again. In a hopeless voice she said, 'Experiment is – necessary, don't you think?'

'You mean that we sometimes become somebody else?'

A squat toadlike figure appeared at Innes' side. 'Why, *Adrian,*' Innes said in that expiring voice. She offered a papery cheek which he touched ceremoniously. Innes made a feeble gesture in Melisande's direction. 'This is —' Her voice died away altogether. Adrian ignored Melisande. She moved away and met Frederick.

He was leaning against a wall with a glass in his hand, a tall man with a brown face, and he gave her at once an impression of reliability. It was connected somehow with his old tweed jacket and his polished shoes, but there was something reassuring even in the way he nodded to her, said hello, and asked if she knew everybody. She replied that she knew nobody at all.

'I'll tell you a secret, neither do I.' His face showed deep creases, like crinkles in well-worn leather, when he smiled. 'And I'll tell you something else. I'm older than anybody else here, and feeling my age. What's your name?'

When she told him he said, 'Beautiful. But rather a mouthful for a practical man like me. I shall call you Melly.'

Somehow she did not feel any resentment when he used the abbreviation, and when he said that his name was Frederick Thomas she thought a moment and then said it suited him.

'I feel that's a criticism,' he said.

For a moment she had trouble in keeping him properly focused. But she blinked and it was all right again.

'If you're a practical man and you don't know anybody –' She lost track of what she wanted to say, then came out with it triumphantly '– why are you here?'

'I'm a computer engineer and I've been helping Gabriel with his last book.'

'The one about – about the machines who had children?'

'That's it. He wanted to make the mechanical details plausible, and they are. A remarkable character, our Gabriel.'

'I work for his publisher.'

He nodded. 'Melly, are you feeling all right?'

'Perfectly.' But the considerate tone in which he spoke almost brought tears to her eyes. 'Only I don't think I like this drink very much.' She gave it to him and he put it on a shelf.

'There's some food over there. Would you like anything?'

She shook her head. 'My name really is Melisande, there's a poem about me. 'Pale little princess, passionate and shy', it begins. Do you know it?'

'I don't read much poetry. I'm afraid I'm an uncultured character. But I'll tell you something, it suits you.'

'I like your jacket.' She touched the rough cloth of it at just the moment when Gabriel clapped his hands.

He stood looking down on them, and her momentary impression was that some act of levitation had been performed. Then she saw that he was standing on a table. His blue eyes glittered, his fair hair hung down over his forehead. She had been aware even in the staid office surroundings of some magnetic quality about him and now this magnetism was intensified so that he looked like a woodland demon.

'We are going to conduct an experiment in personality.' There was a faint murmur from the group, which might have been laughter or excitement. 'I'm not talking about pot or LSD – you know what I think about them, they're simply means of heightening sensation artificially. In the long run they have no meaning, they don't say anything about what you *are*. They turn you on or they don't, all right. But supposing we dispensed with artificiality's aid, could we still turn ourselves on? What sort of people *are* we?'

'Respectable,' somebody said. There was a small ripple of laughter. Gabriel threw back his head and joined it. Melisande looked at his neck, white and smooth. Something about the shape made her uncomfortable. She turned her head and saw Innes. Her eyes were closed, her lips moved as if in prayer.

'All right. Each of us has his own identity, and most of those identities are respectable. But suppose we were anonymous, suppose A were the same as B, supposing all differences of sex were suddenly wiped out –'

'Shame,' somebody said, but there was no laughter.

'– Are you convinced you would be the same person?

Might you not become somebody else?' Gabriel's voice had quickened.

'How are you going to make us anonymous?' That was the underground film man, Bud – what was his last name?

'That's the game. I call it Anonymous People. It's a scientific experiment, but there's one rule. When you're playing, don't speak.' Gabriel paused. 'If people speak, sex differences will be noticed – that's the point. Otherwise, just have fun. One more thing.'

He looked round and they stared up at him expectantly. 'Open your minds to the possible. Don't hold back. Anyone who doesn't want to play, say so.'

Nobody moved. Gabriel paused as though considering whether to say more, then jumped down. Was Innes still praying? She seemed to have disappeared.

'But, Gabriel darling, what do we *do?*' Lenya asked.

Gabriel said mockingly, 'Since you ask, Lenya darling, you can be first. Through there.' He opened a door, which was not the one through which they had come in, gave her a gentle push, closed it again, and stood beside it. 'One at a time.'

Frederick spoke from beside her. 'You said there was only one rule.'

'Yes, once you're on the other side of the door. Except that you don't come back here. There'll be a little wait. I suggest you all pour yourselves another drink.'

Half a dozen people did so, but there was an uneasy silence. After a minute there was a buzz, rather like that heard in a doctor's waiting room. Gabriel jerked a thumb at Bud Masters, who went through the door.

The process was repeated at about the same intervals of time. Once there was a longer waiting period, perhaps of two minutes, and Gabriel opened the door, then quickly closed it again. Beside her Frederick said something.

'What's that?' she asked.

'I don't much like this. He's playing with things he doesn't understand.'

'It's a scientific experiment.' Her words came out slowly.

'It's Gabriel getting his kicks.'

'Frederick,' Gabriel called. Frederick smiled at her, went across to the door, and passed through it.

Now that he had gone she felt very tired. She sat down in an armchair and closed her eyes. Behind them some recollection seemed to burn. She was in a plane which swooped in circles lower and lower toward the ground, the ground becoming bigger, the details of it frighteningly large. Bump, bump, they had landed, but where was her father? He appeared at the door of the plane and swept off his Panama hat with a smile that was not reassuring but mocking. She got up to greet him but something, a pressure on one shoulder, held her back in the seat.

With an effort she opened her eyes. Gabriel's hand was on her shoulder. He said, 'Your turn, baby.' There were only two other people left in the room. He opened the door for her and with a feeling of physical dread she passed through it.

She found herself in Gabriel's study. There was a work chart on one wall, a neat desk beside it. It was all perfectly ordinary, but then what had she expected? And what was she meant to do? A single lamp burned over the desk but some other light disturbed her. Slowly, and again with effort, she swivelled her eyes and saw over a door an extemporized sign with a light behind it, which said in capitals: TAKE OFF SHOES, MEN TAKE OFF JACKETS, PUT ON CLOTHES AND GLOVES, LEAVE BY THIS DOOR.

Now she saw a row of shoes on the floor, looking as though they had been left outside a hotel bedroom; men's jackets were flung on a sofa, a bundle of clothes was beneath the sign. She picked up the clothes. There were three pieces of clothing in each bundle and they were made of rubber. Three-piece suit in rubber, she thought, and checked her laughter. Rubber gloves lay beside the clothes.

The trousers had an elastic waist and slipped on easily after she had taken off her shoes, and the upper part was quite simple too, a sort of rubber windbreaker, again elastic at the waist, which clung in some places and was loose in others. The helmet-style headpiece had holes in the mouth and nostrils through which to breathe, but otherwise it fitted closely.

I must look like something from Mars, she thought and looked round the room to find with a shock that she could hardly see it. The eyepieces of the rubber helmet must have been made of some partly opaque material that made everything look dim. She had to grope rather than walk.

'Come on,' a voice snapped. Gabriel had opened the door from the living room and was looking in. She raised a rubber hand and opened the door below the lighted sign. As she passed through and closed it she heard the buzzer sound.

It was like entering another world. No, no, she thought. I mustn't use a cliché like that; rather it was like being a partially-sighted person, aware of everything yet unable to see properly. She was in a hall, and this must be the entrance hall of the house, but it looked entirely different through these blurry eyepieces.

She opened a door but it seemed to be only that of a closet under the stairs, so she closed it again. The staircase was by her side, a passage loomed ahead, and the element of choice involved in the question 'Which way shall I go?' suddenly seemed important. As slowly as an invalid she made her way along the passage to find at the end of it another flight of stairs leading downwards.

She descended, holding onto the stair rail, and again the loss of tactile sensation because of the rubber suit was disconcerting, although she told herself that it was only like wearing rubber gloves for washing up. At the bottom of the stairs there were three doors. Which one to choose, and where was everybody?

She opened the middle door and made a small sound of surprise when she saw a reflection of herself inside. Then the figure raised a rubber arm and saw another rubber figure holding a knife and she realized that everybody was dressed alike. What was it Gabriel had said – 'supposing A were the same as B' – that was it precisely. The knife descended, carved a slice off some kind of meat that looked like ham, pinned it with the knife, and offered it to her. She was in the kitchen.

She shook her head and the figure began to push the ham through the small breathing slit in the headpiece made for the mouth. She watched with revulsion as the meat disappeared bit by bit rather as though it were being consumed by a snake. Half of the piece of meat dropped off and fell to the floor. With a slight bow the figure offered her the knife and she took it automatically while watching the other man – or woman? – who had opened a refrigerator and was peering inside.

A bottle of milk was ceremoniously taken out, held up, the top removed. For drinking? Unbelievingly she saw the milk – she knew that it was milk although in this dim light the colour was indiscernible – poured onto the floor. Ham-nibbler wagged a reproving finger. Milk-pourer put the empty bottle back into the refrigerator and spread out arms like a conjurer who has performed a successful trick. Melly turned and walked out of the kitchen.

Anonymous people, she thought as she opened a second door which proved to be that of a dining room in which another rubber figure was arranging knives and forks on the table in an elaborate star pattern; I don't like anonymous people. She stumbled a little as she hurried up the stairs thinking, I want to get out of this, I am not an anonymous person.

She went to the door of Gabriel's study and shrank back as another anonymous person came out and passed apparently without seeing her. With one rubber paw on the door handle she remembered that Gabriel had said, 'Don't come back here,' and thought how conspicuous she would make herself by going back. I can play the game for a little while longer, she thought; after all, I don't have to join in and *do* anything. She could find some place in a room and just sit there quietly.

On the second floor she was again confronted by a choice of doors. Like Alice in Wonderland, she thought vaguely, although was it really like Alice? She played a game of her own in front of the doors, saying eeny-meenie-minie-mo to decide which to open. It turned out that she had picked the bathroom, and she shut this door quickly when she saw a rubber figure standing under the shower with water pouring all over it, him, her. The figure capered about at sight of her and she remembered her father saying when she was a small child, 'Come on in, the water's lovely.'

The sense of outrage she felt about the man – it must have been a man, no woman would have done such a thing – came from the feeling that he was doing the wrong action; she could not have put it more precisely than that. When she opened the adjoining door, she entered what turned out to be a bedroom and sat down on a bed; at first she thought there was nobody else in the room and that she had escaped from the world of wrong behaviour.

Then she saw the rubber man – she was prepared, it turned out, to identify all of them as men – sitting at a small writing desk. It took her a moment or two to see what he was doing, and another few seconds before she believed it. He had a screwdriver or chisel in his hand and he was using it to force open the top of the desk. The effect, as the top opened, was rather that of an old silent film, for she saw the splintered wood where the lock had been forced and yet because of the rubber suiting she could hear nothing. But now the sense of outrage was strong enough for her to try to stop him.

She got off the bed and advanced toward the man. He was not aware of her presence until she was almost upon him. Then he jumped up, backed away, turned, and ran out of the door. She did not understand why he had seemed so frightened until she looked down and saw that the knife given to her in the kitchen was still clasped in her rubbery right hand. He had thought an attack was being made on him, and perhaps he was right. Perhaps she would have attacked him with the knife. She might have done the wrong thing too.

The thought was upsetting. She went over to the desk and closed it, resisting the very real temptation to look at the letters she could see inside. I must stop it, she said to herself, and felt that to get away from temptation she must hide. She knew the place for hiding. She hurried out of the bedroom, passed two figures as she ran down the stairs – one of them tried to stop her – reached the ground floor, opened the door of the closet under the stairs, and got inside.

She sat down because there was no room to stand up, pulled the door almost completely shut, and had instantly the most wonderful feeling of safety. She was at once perfectly relaxed and very tired. She put the knife on her knees, leaned back, and closed her eyes. . .

She could not remember afterwards how long she had slept, or indeed whether she had slept at all. The inside of the closet was dark, and it made little difference to what she saw or didn't see whether her eyes were open or closed, as she found when she flapped them up and down like tiny shutters. And it was as she did this flapping – if my eyes were wings, she thought, I could use them to fly – that she became aware of another presence. She did not *hear* – that was not possible – but she knew there was somebody else with her.

Strangely enough, perhaps because of her utter relaxation, she was not frightened. She was prepared for something to happen, yet when it did happen she had at first a feeling of apprehension so that she shifted her body slightly away from the thing that was touching her. The thing moved with her, rippled down her backbone, and she realized its nature. A hand was moving up and down her back.

The activities of the disembodied hand gave her pleasure. It began at the small of her back, moved gently in circles that radiated out from the backbone and rose to the nape of the neck, which reassuringly did not feel like the real nape of a real neck because the whole thing was made of rubber. The effect was soothing; it made her feel at peace, yet one of the agreeable things about it was the undercurrent of excitement, the sense that this was a preliminary activity.

She knew that the body behind her would move closer, and it did. The hand moved round to the front of her body, and just when she was wondering whether this was a one-handed man, the other hand made itself known. The two rubber hands linked together across her middle – how clearly she saw them in her mind's eye! – and then moved upward, upward.

The sensation she experienced then was of a piercing sweetness previously unknown to her. Certainly the affair with clumsy Archie had offered nothing comparable to it. The other body pressed against her own urgently, and the hands now gripped hard where they had previously stroked. She wanted to turn her head but it seemed to be fixed, and what would she see but a mask made of rubber?

The knowledge that no fulfillment was possible heightened her pleasure and even when the hands moved up to her neck, the pleasure remained undiminished. Then the hands tightened and she was struck with panic, trying to turn her head to ease the pressure on her windpipe, twisting to convey that he was pressing too hard, pulling at the hands with her feeble paws, groping for the knife on her knees, and using it to jab upward awkwardly once, twice.

And yet, before she lost consciousness, she wanted to express regret for this action and to make it known somehow that her predominant feeling had been one of pleasure, almost of ecstasy. . .

'Rather a success,' Gabriel said. 'Perhaps it should have been more carefully organized, but still distinctly a success. Several plates and dishes smashed, one desk forced open, one bathroom semi-flooded, three chairs and a small table thrown out of a window. Some odds and ends broken, probably by accident. Would any of you have done such things if you hadn't been anonymous? Of course not. Two regrettable incidents. One couple found removing their suits for extracurricular purposes. I won't name them. And one faint – from heat, I expect. Sorry about that.'

She heard all this very vaguely, but felt the need to protest. 'I didn't faint. Somebody tried to —' She stopped at that. She was lying on the sofa in the sitting room and now she looked up at the faces around her, some anxious and some amused. Gabriel's face was amused. The room wavered. She closed her eyes.

There was a hand on her forehead. A voice said,

'Burning hot. She ought to be in bed.'

She opened her eyes again. 'How did you find me?'

Gabriel answered. 'You were flat out on the floor in the hall, darling. I brought you in here and gave you some brandy.'

'In the hall? Not in the closet under the stairs?'

'The glory hole? No, baby. Were you there?'

'I thought so. Did you find a – a knife?'

He raised his eyebrows, shook his head, and she wondered if he had been the man with her. Articulating with conscious clearness she said, 'I was in what you call the glory hole. You were in there with me, weren't you?'

There was a murmur, one distinctly of amusement. Gabriel said gently, indulgently, 'If you say so. And what happened in the glory hole, baby?'

But what had happened – the burning pleasure she had felt and her intense desire to repeat it – was something she could not say out loud. She shook her head and stared at him. His blue eyes looked back at her searchingly, and his words seemed to have a peculiar emphasis. 'What you've got to remember is that nothing happened, nothing at all. You fainted and I found you on the floor in the hall. Anything else was your imagination.'

She nodded, to show that she was prepared not to accuse him again. Her hand went to her neck, which did not ache or feel sore. Was it true then? Had she imagined it all? She looked wonderingly round at the faces – Bud Masters with his sideburns, monocled Lenya, Bruno Moustache, drooping Innes, and the others. They stared back at her with concern. There was silence, broken by Bruno.

'Can't imagine what you think you've proved, Gabriel. Just got a lot of stuff smashed up, that's all.'

Now Gabriel's gaze shifted from her, and his manner eased. 'I don't set out to prove things. Except to myself. And to Innes perhaps.'

Lenya, hovering beside Melisande, said, 'You look pretty wild, you know. As if you're not really here. Come with me and I'll put you to bed.'

'Not necessary.' That was Gabriel. 'We can easily put you up here, can't we, Innes?'

'No.' The thought of staying in that house terrified her. She saw Frederick's leathery face and spoke to it. 'Please take me home.'

She barely said goodbye to Gabriel and Innes, and did not speak to the rest of them. On the way back in the taxi Frederick said it had been a damned stupid party and that Gabriel was a silly man. She felt too tired to contradict him.

Back in her apartment he said, 'Now, if you can get yourself to bed I'll make some hot milk. Any aspirin about?'

'Yes, but I've got pills —'

'No pills. Just aspirin.'

He sat beside the bed while she drank the milk and aspirin. She waited for him to kiss her, but he only looked at her with dog-brown eyes like her father's. Or had her father's eyes been blue like Gabriel's? It worried her that she could not remember.

'Feeling better?' She felt just the same but said she was better. He spoke earnestly. 'You weren't feeling well enough to go out, and it was terribly hot inside that rubber gear. You fainted and Gabriel found you. Nothing else happened.'

'Nothing else happened,' she echoed like a child, closed her eyes, and was asleep. She felt his lips brush her forehead in a good-night kiss like her father's – or was that a dream too?

On the following morning he phoned to see how she was and asked her out to lunch as soon as she felt up to it, any day, any day at all. She did not really feel up to it, but she had lunch with him that day and dinner the day after. A month later they were married.

Frederick had sufficient money to buy a little house almost in the country, but not too far away from his work. She left the publishing firm because she did not want to see Gabriel again and got a few other secretarial jobs; but Frederick did not want his wife to work and she settled down to becoming a housewife.

He called her Melly because Melisande, he said, was rather ridiculous in this day and age, and she accepted this. Their lovemaking was infrequent, inhibited, and produced no children. Frederick became in time an administrator, in charge of a large department. Melly took up social work connected with juvenile delinquents, which she found interesting. They were good solid citizens, and as their friends used to say, real assets to the community.

Frederick never again mentioned the Anonymous People party to her, and as time went by she felt increasing doubt that anything had happened. Had she imagined it all, or were there other possibilities in her personality that remained unfulfilled? And not only in her personality.

How could she ask if the long deep scratches on Frederick's arm – the scratches she had noticed when he brought her the milk in bed that night – if they had been made by her knife when it tore through the rubber windbreaker? She was willing – or was she? – to bury the events of that evening, so that she never knew whether for one single hour of his life, he – like Melisande – had become somebody else.

The Flowers That Bloom in the Spring

The outsider, Bertie Mays was fond of saying, sees most of the game. In the affair of the Purchases and the visiting cousin from South Africa he saw quite literally all of it. But the end was enigmatic and a little frightening, at least as seen through Bertie's eyes. It left with him the question whether there had been a game at all.

Bertie had retired early from his unimportant and uninteresting job in the Ministry of Welfare. He had a private income, he was unmarried, and his only extravagance was a passion for travel, so why go on working? Bertie gave up his London flat and settled down in the cottage in the Sussex countryside which he had bought years earlier as a weekend place. It was quite big enough for a bachelor, and Mrs Last from the village came in two days a week to clean the place. Bertie himself was an excellent cook.

It was a fine day in June when he called next door to offer Sylvia Purchase a lift to the tea party at the Hall. She was certain to have been asked, and he knew that she would need a lift because he had seen her husband Jimmy putting a case into the boot of their ancient Morris. Jimmy was some sort of freelance journalist, and often went on trips, leaving Sylvia on her own. Bertie, who was flirtatious by nature, had asked if she would like him to keep her company, but she did not seem responsive to the suggestion. Linton House, which the Purchases had rented furnished a few months earlier, was a rambling old place with oak beams and low ceilings. There was an attractive garden, some of which lay between the house and Bertie's cottage, and by jumping over the fence between them

Bertie could walk across this garden. He did so that afternoon, taking a quick peek into the sitting room as he went by. He could never resist such peeks, because he always longed to know what people might be doing when they thought that nobody was watching. On this occasion the sitting room was empty. He found Sylvia in the kitchen, washing dishes in a half-hearted way.

'Sylvia, you're not ready.' She had on a dirty old cardigan with the buttons done up wrongly. Bertie himself was, as always, dressed very suitably for the occasion in a double-breasted blue blazer with brass buttons, fawn trousers and a neat bow tie. He always wore bow ties, which he felt gave a touch of distinction and individuality.

'Ready for what?'

'Has the Lady of the Manor not bidden you to tea?' That was his name for Lady Hussey up at the Hall.

She clapped hand to forehead, leaving a slight smudge. 'I'd forgotten all about it. Don't think I'll go, can't stand those bun fights.'

'But I have called specially to collect you. Let me be your chauffeur. Your carriage awaits.' Bertie made a sketch of a bow, and Sylvia laughed. She was a blonde in her early thirties, attractive in a slapdash sort of way.

'Bertie, you are a fool. All right, give me five minutes.'

The women may call Bertie Mays a fool, Bertie thought, but how they adore him.

'Oh,' Sylvia said. She was looking behind Bertie, and when he turned he saw a man standing in the shadow of the door. At first glance he thought it was Jimmy, for the man was large and square like Jimmy, and had the same gingery fair colouring. But the resemblance went no further, for as the man stepped forward he saw that their features were not similar.

'This is my cousin Alfred Wallington. He's paying us a visit from South Africa. Our next door neighbour, Bertie Mays.'

'Pleased to meet you.' Bertie's hand was firmly gripped. The two men went into the sitting room, and Bertie asked whether this was Mr Wallington's first visit.

'By no means. I know England pretty well. The south, anyway.'

'Ah, business doesn't take you up north?' Bertie thought of himself as a tactful but expert interrogator, and the question should have brought a response telling him Mr Wallington's occupation. In fact, however, the other man merely said that was so.

'In the course of my work I used to correspond with several firms in Cape Town,' Bertie said untruthfully. Wallington did not comment. 'Is your home near there?'

'No.'

The negative was so firm that it gave no room for further conversational manoeuvre. Bertie felt slightly cheated. If the man did not want to say where he lived in South Africa of course he was free to say nothing, but there was a certain finesse to be observed in such matters, and a crude 'no' was not at all the thing. He was able to establish at least that this was the first time Wallington had visited Linton House

On the way up to the Hall he said to Sylvia that her cousin seemed a dour fellow.

'Alf?' Bertie winced at the abbreviation. 'He's all right when you get to know him.'

'He said he was often in the south. What's his particular sphere of interest?'

'I don't know, I believe he's got some sort of export business around Durban. By the way, Bertie, how did you know Jimmy was away?'

'I saw him waving goodbye to you.' It would hardly do to say that he had been peeping through the curtains.

'Did you now? I was in bed when he went. You're a bit of a fibber I'm afraid, Bertie.'

'Oh, I can't remember *how* I knew.' Really, it was too much to be taken up on every little point.

When they drove into the great courtyard and Sylvia got out of the car, however, he reflected that she looked very slenderly elegant, and that he was pleased to be with her. Bertie liked pretty women and they were safe with him, although he would not have thought of it that way. He might have said, rather, that he would never have compromised a lady, with the implication that all sorts of things might be said and done providing that they stayed within the limits of discretion. It occurred to him that Sylvia was hardly staying within those limits when she allowed herself to be alone at Linton House with her South African cousin. Call me old-fashioned, Bertie said to himself, but I don't like it.

The Hall was a nineteenth century manor house and by no means, as Bertie had often said, an architectural gem, but the lawns at the back where tea was served were undoubtedly fine. Sir Reginald Hussey was a building contractor who had been knighted for some dubious service to the export drive. He was in demand for opening fêtes and fund-raising enterprises, and the Husseys entertained a selection of local people to parties of one kind or another half a dozen times a year. The parties were always done in style, and this afternoon there were maids in white caps and aprons, and a kind of major domo who wore a frock coat and white gloves. Sir Reginald was not in evidence, but Lady Hussey presided in a regal manner.

Of course Bertie knew that it was all ridiculously vulgar and ostentatious, but still he enjoyed himself. He kissed Lady Hussey's hand and said that the scene was quite entrancing, like a Victorian period picture, and he had an interesting chat with Lucy Broadhinton, who was the widow of an Admiral. Lucy was the president and Bertie the secretary of the local historical society, and they were great friends. She told him now in the strictest secrecy about the outrageous affair Mrs Monro was having with somebody who must be nameless, although from the details given Bertie was quite able to guess his identity. There were other titbits too, like the story of the scandalous misuse of the Church Restoration Fund money. It was an enjoyable afternoon, and he fairly chortled about it on the way home.

'They're such snobby affairs,' Sylvia said. 'I don't know why I went.'

'You seemed to be having a good time. I was quite jealous.'

Sylvia had been at the centre of a very animated circle of three or four young men. Her laughter at their jokes had positively rung out across the lawns, and Bertie had seen Lady Hussey give more than one disapproving glance in the direction of the little group. There was something undeniably attractive about Sylvia's gaiety and about the way in which she threw back her head when laughing, but her activities had a recklessness about them which was not proper for a lady. He tried to convey something of this as he drove back, but was not sure that she understood what he meant. He also broached delicately the impropriety of her being alone in the house with her cousin by asking when Jimmy would be coming back. In a day or two, she said casually. He refused her invitation to come in for a drink. He had no particular wish to see Alf Wallington again.

On the following night at about midnight, when Bertie was in bed reading, he heard a car draw up next door. Doors were closed, there was the sound of voices. Just to confirm that Jimmy was back, Bertie got out of bed and lifted an edge of the curtain. A man and a woman were coming out of the garage. The woman was Sylvia. The man had his arm round her, and as Bertie watched bent down and kissed her neck. Then they moved towards the front door, and the man laughed and said something. From his general build he might, seen in the dim light, have been Jimmy, but the voice had the distinctive South African accent of Wallington.

Bertie drew away from the window as though he had been scalded.

It was a feeling of moral responsibility that took him round to Linton House on the following day. To his surprise Jimmy Purchase opened the door.

'I – ah – thought you were away.'

'Got back last night. What can I do for you?'

Bertie said that he would like to borrow the electric hedge clippers, which he knew were in the garden shed. Jimmy led the way there and handed them over. Bertie said that he had heard the car coming back at about midnight.

'Yeah.' Jimmy had a deplorably Cockney voice, not at all out of the top drawer. 'That was Sylvia and Alf. He took her to a dance over at Ladersham. I was too fagged out, just wanted to get my head down.'

'Her cousin from South Africa?'

'Yeah, right, from the Cape. He's staying here for a bit. Plenty of room.'

Was he from the Cape or from Durban? Bertie did not fail to notice the discrepancy.

Bertie's bump of curiosity was even stronger than his sense of propriety. It became important, even vital, that he should know just what was going on next door. When he returned the hedge cutters he asked them all to dinner, together with Lucy Broadhinton to make up the number. He took pains in preparing a delicious cold meal. The salmon was cooked to perfection, and the hollandaise sauce had just the right hint of something tart beneath its blandness.

The evening was not a success. Lucy had on a long dress and Bertie wore a very smart velvet jacket, but Sylvia was dressed in sky blue trousers and a vivid shirt, and the two men wore open-necked shirts and had distinctly unkempt appearances. They had obviously been drinking before they arrived. Wallington tossed down Bertie's expensive hock as though it were water, and then said that South African wine had more flavour than that German stuff.

'You're from Durban, I believe, Mr Wallington.' Lucy fixed him with her Admiral's lady glance. 'My husband and I were there in the sixties, and thought it delightful. Do you happen to know the Morrows or the Page-Manleys? Mary Page-Manley gave such delightful parties.'

Wallington looked at her from under heavy brows. 'Don't know them.'

'You have an export business in Durban?'

'That's right.'

There was an awkward pause. Then Sylvia said, 'Alf's trying to persuade us to pay him a visit out there.'

'I'd like you to come out. Don't mind about him.' Wallington jerked a thumb at Jimmy. 'Believe me, we'd have a good time.'

'I do believe you, Alf.' She gave her head-back laugh, showing the fine column of her neck. 'It's something we've forgotten here, how to have a good time.'

Jimmy Purchase had been silent during dinner. Now he said, 'People here just don't have the money. Like the song says, it's money makes the world go round.'

'The trouble in Britain is that too much money has got into the wrong hands.' Lucy looked round the table. Nobody seemed inclined to argue the point. 'There are too many grubby little people with sticky fingers.'

'I wish some of the green stuff would stick to my fingers,' Jimmy said, and hiccupped. Bertie realised with horror that he was drunk. 'We're broke, Sylvie, old girl.'

'Oh, shut up.'

'You don't believe me?' And he actually began to empty out his pockets. What appalling creatures the two men were, each as bad as the other. Bertie longed for the evening to end, and was delighted when Lucy rose to make a stately departure. He whispered an apology in the hall, but she told him not to be foolish, it had been fascinating.

When he returned Wallington said, 'What an old battle-axe. *Did you happen to know the Page-Manleys.* Didn't know they were still around, people like that.'

Sylvia was looking at Bertie. 'Alf, you're shocking our host.'

'Sorry, man, but honest, I thought they kept her sort in museums. Stuffed.'

'You mustn't say stuffed. That'll shock Bertie too.'

Bertie said stiffly, 'I am not in the least shocked, but I certainly regard it as the height of bad manners to criticise a guest in such a manner. Lucy is a very dear friend of mine.'

Sylvia at least had some understanding of his feelings. She said sorry and smiled, so that he was at once inclined to forgive her. Then she said it was time she took her rough diamonds home.

'Thanks for the grub,' Wallington said. Then he leaned across the dining table and shouted, 'Wake up, man, it's tomorrow morning already.' Jimmy had fallen asleep in his chair. He was hauled to his feet and supported across the garden.

Bertie called up Lucy the next morning and apologised again. She said that he should think no more about it. 'I didn't take to that South African feller, though. Shouldn't be surprised if he turns out to be a bad hat. And I didn't care too much for your neighbours, if you don't mind my being frank.'

Bertie said of course not, although he reflected that there seemed to be a sudden spasm of frankness among his acquaintances. Mrs Purchase, Lucy said, had a roving eye. She left it at that, and they went on to discuss the agenda for the next meeting of the historical society.

Later in the morning there was a knock on the door. Jimmy was there, hollow-eyed and slightly green. ''Fraid we rather blotted our copybook last night. Truth is, Alf and I were fairly well loaded before we came round. Can't remember too much about it, but Syl said apologies were in order.'

Bertie asked when Sylvia's cousin was leaving. Jimmy Purchase shrugged and said he didn't know. Bertie nearly said that the man should not be left alone with Sylvia, but refrained. He might be inquisitive, but he was also discreet.

A couple of nights later he was doing some weeding in the garden when he heard voices raised in Linton House. One was Jimmy's, the other belonged to Sylvia. They were in the sitting room shouting at each other, not quite loudly enough for the words to be distinguishable. It was maddening not to know what was being said. Bertie moved along the fence separating the gardens, until he was as near as he could get without being seen. He was now able to hear a few phrases.

'Absolutely sick of it . . . drink because it takes my mind off . . . told you we have to wait. . .' That was Jimmy. Then Sylvia's voice, shrill as he had never heard it, shrill and sneering.

'Tell me the old old story. . . how long do we bloody well wait then. . . you said it would be finished by now.' An indistinguishable murmur from Jimmy. 'None of your business,' she said. More murmuring. 'None of your business what I do.' Murmur murmur. 'You said yourself we're broke.' To this there was some reply. Then she said clearly, 'I shall do what I like.'

'*All right*' Jimmy said, so loudly that Bertie fairly jumped. There followed a sharp crack, which sounded like hand on flesh.

Sylvia said, 'You bastard, that's it, then.'

Nothing more. No sound, no speech. Bertie waited five minutes and then tiptoed away, fearful of being seen. Once indoors again he felt quite shaky, and had to restore himself by a nip of brandy. What had the conversation meant? Much of it was plain enough. Sylvia was saying that it was none of her husband's business if she carried on an affair. But what was it they had to wait for, what was it that should have been finished? A deal connected with the odious Alf? And where was Alf, who as Bertie had noticed went out into the village very little?

He slept badly, and was wakened in the middle of the night by a piercing, awful scream. He sat up in bed quivering, but the sound was not repeated. He decided that he must have been dreaming.

On the following day the car was not in the garage. Had Jimmy gone off again? He met Sylvia out shopping in the village, and she said that he had been called to an assignment at short notice.

'What sort of assignment?' He had asked before for the name of the paper Jimmy worked on, to be told that he was a freelance.

'A Canadian magazine. He's up in the Midlands, may be away a few days.'

Should he say something about the row? But that would have been indiscreet, and in any case Sylvia had such a wild look in her eye that he did not care to ask further questions. It was on this morning that he read about the Small Bank Robbers.

The Small Bank Robbers had been news for some months. They specialised in fast, well organised raids on banks, and had carried out nearly twenty of these in the past year. Several men were involved in each raid. They were armed, and did not hesitate to use coshes or revolvers when necessary. In one bank a screaming woman customer had suffered a fractured skull when hit over the head, and in another a guard who resisted the robbers had been shot and killed. The diminutive applied to them referred to the banks they robbed, not to their own physical dimensions. A bank clerk who admitted giving information to the gang had asked why they were interested in his small branch bank, and had been told that they always raided small banks because they were much more vulnerable than large ones. After the arrest of this clerk the robbers seemed to have gone to ground. There had been no news of them for the last three or four weeks.

Bertie had heard about the Small Bank Robbers, but took no particular interest in them. He was a nervous man, and did not care for reading about crime. On this morning, however, his eye was caught by the heading: *Small Bank Robbers. The South African Connection.* The story was a feature by the paper's crime reporter, Derek Holmes. He said that Scotland Yard knew the identities of some of the robbers, and described his own investigations, which led to the conclusion that three or four of them were in Spain. The article continued:

> *But there is another connection, and a sinister one. The men in Spain are small fry. My researches suggest that the heavy men who organised the robberies, and were very ready to use violence, came from South Africa. They provided the funds and the muscle. Several witnesses who heard the men talking to each other or giving orders during the raids have said that they used odd accents. This has been attributed to the sound distortion caused by the stocking masks they wore, but two men I spoke to, both of whom have spent time in*

South Africa, said that they had no doubt the accent was South African.

The writer suggested that these men were now probably back in South Africa. But supposing that one of them was still in England, that he knew Jimmy and Sylvia and had a hold over them? Supposing, even, that they were minor members of the gang themselves? The thought made Bertie shiver with fright and excitement. What should or could he do about it? And where had Jimmy Purchase gone?

Again he slept badly, and when he did fall into a doze it was a short one. He woke to find Wallington knocking on the door. Once inside the house he drew out a huge wad of notes, said that there was enough for everybody, and counted out bundles which he put on the table between them with a small decisive *thwack*. A second bundle, *thwack*, and a third, *thwack*. How many more? He tried to cry out, to protest, but the bundles went on, *thwack, thwack, thwack*. . .

He sat up in bed, crying out something inaudible. The thin grey light of early morning came through the curtains. There was a sound in the garden outside, a sound regularly repeated, the *thwack* of his dream. It took him in his slightly dazed state a little while to realise that if he went to the window he might see what was causing the sound. He tiptoed across the room and raised the curtain. He was trembling.

It was still almost dark, and whatever was happening was taking place at the back of Linton House, so that he could not see it. But as he listened to the regularly repeated sound, he had no doubt of its nature. Somebody was digging out there. The sound of the spade digging earth had entered his dream, and there was an occasional clink when it struck a stone. Why would somebody be digging at this time in the morning? He remembered that terrible cry on the previous night, the cry he had thought to be a dream. Supposing it had been real, who had cried out?

The digging stopped and two people spoke, although he could not hear the words or even the tones. One, light and high in pitch, was no doubt Sylvia, but was the other voice Wallington's? And if it was, had Jimmy Purchase gone away at all? In the half light a man and woman were briefly visible before they passed into the house. The man carried a spade, but his head was down and Bertie could not see his face, only his square bulky figure. He had little doubt that the man was Wallington.

That morning he went up to London. He had visited the city rarely since his retirement, finding that on each visit he was more worried and confused. The place seemed continually to change, so that what had been a landmark of some interest was a kebab or hamburger restaurant. The article had appeared in the *Banner*, and their offices had moved from Fleet Street to somewhere off the Gray's Inn Road. He asked for Arnold Grayson, a deputy editor he had known slightly, to be told that Grayson had moved to another paper. He had to wait almost an hour before he was able to talk to Derek Holmes. The crime reporter remained staring at his desk while he listened to Bertie's story. During the telling of it he chewed gum and said 'Yup' occasionally.

'Yup,' he said again at the end. 'Okay, Mr Mays. Thanks.'

'What are you going to do about it?'

Holmes removed his gum and considered the question. 'Know how many people been in touch about that piece, saying they've seen the robbers, their landlord's one of them, they heard two South Africans talking in a bus about how the loot should be split, etcetera? One hundred and eleven. Half of 'em are sensationalists, the other half plain crazy.'

'But this is different.'

'They're all different. I shouldn'ta seen you only you mentioned Arnie, and he was a good friend. But what's it amount to? Husband and wife have a shindig, husband goes off, South African cousin's digging a flowerbed —'

'At that time in the morning?'

The reporter shrugged. 'People are funny.'

'Have you got pictures of the South Africans you say are involved in the robberies? If I could recognise Wallington —'

Holmes put another piece of gum in his mouth, chewed on it meditatively, and then produced half a dozen photographs. None of them resembled Wallington. Holmes shuffled the pictures together, put them away. 'That's it then.'

'But aren't you going to come down and look into it? I tell you I believe murder has been done. Wallington is her lover. Together they have killed Purchase.'

'If Wallington's lying low with his share of the loot, the last thing he'd do is get involved in this sort of caper. You know your trouble, Mr Mays? You've got an overheated imagination.'

If only he knew somebody at Scotland Yard! But there was no reason to think that they would take him any more seriously than the newspaper man had done. He returned feeling both chastened and frustrated. To his surprise Sylvia got out of another carriage on the train. She greeted him cheerfully.

'Hallo Bertie. I've just been seeing Alf off.'

'Seeing Alf off?' he echoed stupidly.

'Back to South Africa. He had a letter saying they needed him back there.'

'Back in Durban?'

'That's right.'

'Jimmy said he was from the Cape.'

'Did he? Jimmy often gets things wrong.'

It was not in Bertie's nature to be anything but gallant to a lady, even one he suspected of being a partner in murder. 'Now that you are a grass widow again, you must come in and have a dish of tea.'

'That would be lovely.'

'Tomorrow?'

'It's a date.'

They had reached his cottage. She pressed two fingers to her lips, touched his cheek with them. Inside the cottage the telephone was ringing. It was Holmes.

'Mr Mays? Thought you'd like to know. Your chum Purchase is just what he said, a freelance journalist. One or two of the boys knew him. Not too successful from what I hear.'

'So you did pay some attention to what I told you,' Bertie said triumphantly.

'Always try and check a story out. Nothing to this one, far as I can see.'

'Wallington has gone back to South Africa. Suddenly, just like that.'

'Has he now? Good luck to him.'

Triumph was succeeded by indignation. He put down the telephone without saying goodbye.

Was it all the product of an overheated imagination? He made scones for Sylvia's visit next day, and served them with his homemade blackcurrant conserve. Then he put the question that still worried him. He would have liked to introduce it delicately, but somehow didn't manage that.

'What was all that digging in the garden early the other morning?'

Sylvia looked startled, and then exclaimed as a fragment of the scone she was eating dropped on to her dress. When it had been removed she said, 'Sorry you were disturbed. It was Timmy.'

'Timmy?'

'Our tabby. He must have eaten something poisoned and he died. Poor Timmy. Alf dug a grave and we gave him Christian burial.' With hardly a pause she went on, 'We're clearing out at the end of the week.'

'Leaving?' For a moment he could hardly believe it.

'Right. I'm a London girl at heart you know, always was. The idea of coming here was that Jimmy would be able to do some writing of his own, but that never seemed to work out, he was always being called away. If I'm in London I can get a job, earn some money. Very necessary at the moment. If Alf hadn't helped out, I don't know what we'd have done. It was a crazy idea coming down here, but then we're crazy people.'

And at the end of the week Sylvia went. Since the house had been rented furnished, she had only suitcases to take away. She came to say goodbye. There was no sign of Jimmy, and Bertie asked about him.

'Still up on that job. But anyway he wouldn't have wanted to come down and help, he hates things like that. Goodbye, Bertie, we'll meet again I expect.' A quick kiss on the cheek and she was driving off in her hired car.

She departed leaving all sorts of questions unanswered when Bertie came to think about it, mundane ones like an address if anybody should want to get in touch with her or with Jimmy, and things he would have liked to know, such as the reason for digging the cat's grave at such an extraordinary hour. He found himself more and more suspicious of the tale she had told. The row he had overheard could perhaps be explained by lack of money, but it seemed remarkable that Jimmy Purchase had not come back. Linton House was locked up and empty, but it was easy enough to get into the garden. The area dug up was just inside the boundary fence. It was difficult to see how much had been dug because there were patches of earth at either side, but it looked a large area to bury a cat.

On impulse one day, a week after Sylvia had gone, Bertie took a spade into the garden and began to dig. It proved to be quite hard work, and he went down two feet before reaching the body. It was that of a cat, one he vaguely remembered seeing in the house, but Sylvia's story of its death had been untrue. Its head was mangled, shattered by one or two heavy blows.

Bertie looked at the cat with distaste – he did not care for seeing dead things – returned it, and had just finished shovelling back the earth when he was hailed from the road. He turned, and with a sinking heart saw the local constable, P.C.Harris, standing beside his bicycle.

'Ah, it's you, Mr Mays. I was thinking it might be somebody with burglarious intent. Somebody maybe was going to dig a tunnel to get entrance into the house. But perhaps it was your *own* house you was locked out of.' P.C.Harris was well known as a local wag, and nobody laughed more loudly at his own jokes. He laughed heartily now. Bertie joined in feebly.

'But what *was* you doing digging in the next door garden, may I ask?'

What could he say? I was digging for a man, but only found a cat? Desperately Bertie said, 'I'd – ah – lost something and thought it might have got in here. I was just turning the earth.'

The constable shook his head. 'You was trespassing, Mr Mays. This is not your property.'

'No, of course not. It won't happen again. I'd be glad if you could forget it.' He approached the constable, a pound note in his hand.

'No need for that, sir, which might be construed as a bribe and hence an offence in itself. I shall not be reporting the matter on this occasion, nor enquiring further into the whys and wherefores, but would strongly advise you in future to keep within the bounds of your own property.'

Pompous old fool, Bertie thought, but said that of course he would do just that. He scrambled back into his own garden, aware that he made a slightly ludicrous figure. P.C.Harris mounted his bicycle in a stately manner and rode away.

That was almost, but not quite, the end of the story. Linton House was empty for a few weeks and then let again, to a family called Hobson who had two noisy children. Bertie had as little to do with them as possible. He was very conscious of having been made to look a fool, and there was nothing he disliked more than that. He was also aware of a disinclination in himself to enter Linton House again.

In the late spring of the following year he went to Sardinia for a holiday, driving around on his own, looking at the curious nuraghi and the burial places made from gigantic blocks of stone which are called the tombs of the giants. He drove up the western coast in a leisurely way, spending long mornings and afternoons over lunches and dinners in the small towns, and then moving inland to bandit country. He was sitting nursing a drink in a square at Nuoro, which is the capital of the central province, when he heard his name called.

It was Sylvia, so brown that he hardly recognised her. 'Bertie, what are you doing here?'

He said that he was on holiday, and returned the question.

'Just come down to shop. We have a house up in the hills, you must come and see it. Darling, look who's here.'

A bronzed Jimmy Purchase approached across the square. Like Sylvia he seemed in fine spirits, and endorsed enthusiastically the suggestion that Bertie should come out to their house. It was a few miles from the city on the slopes of Mount Ortobene, a long low white modern house at the end of a rough track. They sat in a courtyard and ate grilled fish, with which they drank a hard dry local white wine. Bertie felt his natural curiosity rising. How could he ask questions without appearing to be – well – nosey? Over coffee he said that he supposed Jimmy was out here on an assignment.

It was Sylvia who answered. 'Oh no, he's given all that up since the book was published.'

'The book?'

'Show him, Jimmy.' Jimmy went into the house. He returned with a book which said on the cover *My Tempestuous Life.* As told by Anita Sorana to Jimmy Purchase.

'You've heard of her?'

It would have been difficult not to have heard of Anita Sorana. She was a screen actress famous equally for her temperament, her five well-publicised marriages, and the variety of her love affairs.

'It was fantastic luck when she agreed that Jimmy should write her autobiography. It was all very hush hush and we had to pretend that he was off on assignments when he was really with Anita.'

Jimmy took it up. 'Then she'd break appointments, say she wasn't in the mood to talk. A few days afterwards she'd ask to see me at a minute's notice. Then Sylvia started to play up —'

'I thought he was having an affair with her. She certainly fancied him. He swears he wasn't, but I don't know. Anyway, it was worth it.' She yawned.

'The book was a success?'

Jimmy grinned, teeth very white in his brown face. 'I'll say. Enough for me to shake off the dust of Fleet Street.'

So the quarrel was explained, and Jimmy's sudden

absences, and his failure to return. After a glass of some fiery local liqueur Bertie felt soporific, conscious that he had drunk a little more than usual. There was some other question he wanted to ask, but he did not remember it until they were driving him down the mountain, back to his hotel in Nuoro.

'How is your cousin?'

Jimmy was driving. 'Cousin?'

'Mr Wallington, Sylvia's cousin from South Africa.'

Sylvia, from the back of the car, said 'Alf's dead.'

'Dead!'

'In a car accident. Soon after he got back to South Africa. Wasn't it sad?'

Very few more words were spoken before they reached the hotel and said goodbye. The heat of the hotel room and the wine he had drunk made him fall asleep at once. After a couple of hours he woke, sweating, and wondered if he believed what he had been told. Was it possible to make enough money from 'ghosting' (he had heard that was the word) a life story to retire to Sardinia? It seemed unlikely. He lay on his back in the dark room, and it seemed to him that he saw with terrible clarity what had happened.

Wallington was one of the Small Bank Robbers, and he had come to the Purchases looking for a safe place to stay. He had his money, what Holmes had called the loot, with him, and they had decided to kill him for it. The quarrel had been about when Wallington would be killed, the sound that wakened him in the night had been Wallington's death cry. Jimmy had merely pretended to go away that night, and had returned to help Sylvia dispose of the body. Jimmy dug the grave and they put Wallington in it. Then the cat had been killed and put into a shallow grave on top of the body. It was the killing of the cat, those savage blows on its head, that somehow horrified Bertie most.

He cut short his holiday, took the next plane back. At home he walked round to the place where he had dug up the cat. The Hobsons had put in bedding plants, and the wallflowers were flourishing. He had read somewhere that flowers always flourished over a grave.

'Not thinking of trespassing again, I hope, Mr Mays?'

It was P.C.Harris, red faced and jovial.

Bertie shook his head. What he had imagined in the hotel room might be true, but then again it might not. Supposing that he went to the police, supposing he was able to convince them that there was something in his story, supposing they dug up the flower bed and found nothing but the cat? He would be the laughing stock of the neighbourhood.

Bertie Mays knew that he would say nothing.

'I reckon you was feeling a little bit eccentric that night you was doing the digging,' P.C.Harris said sagely.

'Yes, I think I must have been.'

'They make a fine show, them wallflowers. Makes you more cheerful, seeing spring flowers.'

'Yes', said Bertie Mays meekly. 'They make a fine show.'

THE BOILER

Harold Boyle was on his way out to lunch when the encounter took place that changed his life. He was bound for a vegetarian restaurant, deliberately chosen because to reach it he had to walk across the park. A walk during the day did you good, just as eating a nut, raisin and cheese salad was better for you than consuming chunks of meat that lay like lead in the stomach. He always returned feeling positively healthier, ready and even eager for the columns of figures that awaited him.

On this day he was walking along by the pond, stepping it out to reach the restaurant, when a man coming towards him said 'Hallo.' Harold gave a half-smile, half-grimace, intended as acknowledgement while suggesting that in fact they didn't know each other. The man stopped. He was a fleshy fellow, with a large aggressive face. When he smiled, as he did now, he revealed a mouthful of beautiful white teeth. His appearance struck some disagreeable chord in Harold's memory. Then the man spoke, and the past came back.

'If it isn't the boiler,' he said. 'Jack Cutler, remember me?'

Harold's smallish white hand was gripped in a large red one.

From that moment onwards things seemed to happen of their own volition. He was carried along on the tide of Cutler's boundless energy. The feeble suggestion that he already had a lunch engagement was swept aside, they were in a taxi and then at Cutler's club, and he was having a drink at the bar although he never took liquor at lunchtime. Then lunch, and it turned out that Cutler had ordered already, great steaks that must have cost a fortune, and a bottle of wine with them. During the meal Cutler talked about the firm of building contractors he ran and of its success, the way business was waiting for you if you had the nerve to go out and get it. While he talked, the large teeth bit into the steak as though they were shears. Then his plate was empty.

'Talking about myself too much, always do when I eat. Can't tell you how good it is to see you, my old boiler. What are you doing with yourself?'

'I am a contract estimator for a firm of paint manufacturers.'

'Work out price details, keep an eye open to make sure nobody's cheating? Everybody cheats nowadays, you know that. I reckon some of my boys are robbing me blind, fiddling estimates, taking a cut themselves. You reckon something can be done about that sort of thing?'

'If the estimates are properly checked in advance, certainly.'

Cutler chewed a toothpick. 'What do they pay you at the paint shop?'

It was at this point, he knew afterwards, that he should have said no, he was not interested, he would be late back at the office. Perhaps he should even have been bold enough to tell the truth, and say that he did not want to see Cutler again. Instead he meekly gave the figure.

'Skinflints, aren't they? Come and work for me and I'll double it.'

Again, he knew that he should have said no, I don't want to work for you. Instead, he murmured something about thinking it over.

'That's my good old careful boiler,' Cutler said, and laughed.

'I must get back to the office. Thank you for lunch.'

'You'll be in touch?'

Harold said yes, intending to write a note turning down the offer. When he got home, however, he was foolish enough to mention the offer to his wife, in response to a question about what kind of day he had had. He could have bitten out his tongue the moment after. Of course, she immediately said that he must take it.

'But Phyl, I can't. I don't like Cutler.'

'He seems to like you, taking you to lunch and making this offer. Where did you know him?'

'We were at school together. He likes power over people, that's all he thinks of. He was an awful bully. When we were at school he called me a boiler.'

'A *what*? Oh, I see, a joke on your name. I don't see there's much harm in that.'

'It wasn't a joke. It was to show his – his contempt. He made other people be contemptuous too. And he still says it, when we met he said, it's the boiler.'

'It sounds a bit childish to me. You're not a child now, Harold.'

'You don't understand,' he cried in despair. 'You just don't understand.'

'I'll tell you what I do understand,' she said. Her small pretty face was distorted with anger. 'We've been married eight years, and you've been in the same firm all the time. Same firm, same job, no promotion. Now you're offered double the money. Do you know what that would mean? I could get some new clothes, we could have a washing machine, we might even be able to move out of this neighbourhood to somewhere really nice. And you just say no to it, like that. If you want me to stay you'd better change your mind.'

She went out, slamming the door. When he went upstairs later he found the bedroom door locked. He slept in the spare room.

Or at least he lay in bed there. He thought about Cutler,

who had been a senior when he was a junior. Cutler was the leader of a group who called themselves the Razors, and one day Harold found himself surrounded by them while on his way home. They pushed and pulled him along to the house of one boy whose parents were away. In the garden shed there they held a kind of trial in which they accused him of having sneaked on a gang member who had asked Harold for the answers to some exam questions. Harold had given the answers, some of them had been wrong, and the master had spotted these identical wrong answers. Under questioning, Harold told the master what had happened.

He tried to explain that this was not sneaking, but the gang remained unimpressed. Suggestions about what should be done to him varied from cutting off all his hair to holding him face down in a lavatory bowl. Somebody said that Boyle should be put in a big saucepan and boiled, which raised a laugh. Then Cutler intervened. He was big even then, a big red-faced boy, very sarcastic.

'We don't want to *do* anything, he'll only go snivelling back to teacher. Let's call him something. Call him the boiler.'

Silence. Somebody said, 'Don't see he'll mind.'

'Oh yes, he will.' Cutler came close to Harold, his big face sneering. 'Because I'll tell him what it means, and then he'll remember every time he hears it. Now, you just repeat this after me, boiler.' Then Cutler recited the ritual of the boiler and Harold, after his hair had been pulled and his arm twisted until he thought it would break, repeated it. He remembered the ritual. It began: *I am a boiler. A boiler is a mean little sneak. A boiler's nose is full of snot. He can't tie his own shoelaces. A boiler fails in everything he tries. A boiler stinks. I am a boiler. . .*

Then they let him go, and he ran home. But that was the beginning of it, not the end. Cutler and his gang never called him anything else. They clamped their fingers to their noses when he drew near, and said, 'Watch out, here's the boiler, pooh, what a stink.'

Other boys caught on and did the same. He became a joke, an outcast. His work suffered, he got a bad end of term report. His father had died when he was five, so it was his beloved mother who asked him whether something was wrong. He burst into tears. She said that he must try harder next term, and he shook his head.

'It's no good, I can't. I can't do it, I'm a boiler.'

'A boiler? What do you mean?'

'A boiler, it means I'm no good, can't do anything right. It's what they call me.'

'Who calls you that?'

He told her. She insisted on going up to school and seeing the headmaster, although he implored her not to, and afterwards of course things were worse than ever. The head had said that he would see what could be done, but that boys would be boys and Harold was perhaps oversensitive. Now the gang pretended to burst into tears whenever they saw him, and said poor little boiler should run home to mummy.

And he often did run home from school to mummy. He was not ashamed to remember that he had loved his mother more than anybody else in the world, and that his love had been returned. She was a highly emotional woman, and so nervous that she kept a tiny pearl-handled revolver beside her bed. Harold had lived with her until she died. She left him all she had, which was a little money in gilt edged stocks, some old fashioned jewellery, and the revolver. He sold the stocks and the jewellery, and kept the revolver in a bureau which he used as a writing desk.

It was more than twenty years ago that Cutler had christened him boiler, but the memory remained painful. And now Phyllis wanted him to work with the man. Of course she couldn't know what the word meant, how could anybody know? He saw that in a way Phyllis was right. She had been only twenty-two, ten years younger than Harold, when they were married after his mother's death. It was true that he had expected promotion, he should have changed jobs, it would be wonderful to have more money. You mustn't be a boiler all your life, he said to himself. Cutler was being friendly when he offered you the job.

And he couldn't bear to be on bad terms with Phyl, or to think that she might leave him. There had been an awful time, four years ago, when he had discovered that she was carrying on an affair with another man, some salesman who had called at the door to sell a line in household brooms and brushes. He had come home early one day and found them together. Phyl was shamefaced but defiant, saying that if he only took her out a bit more it wouldn't have happened. Was it the fact that the salesman was a man of her own age, he asked. She shook her head, but said that it might help if Harold didn't behave like an old man of sixty.

In the morning he told Phyl that he had thought it over, and changed his mind. She said that he would have been crazy not to take the job. Later that day he telephoned Cutler.

To his surprise he did not find the new job disagreeable. It was more varied than his old work, and more interesting. He checked everything carefully, as he had always done, and soon unearthed evidence showing that one of the foremen was working with a sales manager to inflate the cost of jobs by putting in false invoices billed to a non-existent firm. Both men were sacked immediately.

He saw Cutler on most days. Harold's office overlooked the entrance courtyard, so that if he looked out of the window he could see Cutler's distinctive gold and silver coloured Rolls draw up. A smart young chauffeur opened the door and the great man stepped out, often with a cigar in his mouth, and nodded to the chauffeur who then took the car round to the parking lot. Cutler came in around ten thirty, and often invaded Harold's office after lunch smelling of drink, his face very red. He was delighted by the discovery of the invoice fraud, and clapped Harold on the back.

'Well done, my old boiler. It was a stroke of inspiration asking you to come here. Hasn't worked out too badly for you either, has it?' Harold agreed. He talked as little as possible to his employer. One day Cutler complained of this.

'Damn it, man, anybody would think we didn't know each other. Just because I use a Rolls and have young Billy Meech drive me in here every morning doesn't mean I'm standoffish. You know why I do it? The Rolls is good publicity, the best you can have, and I get driven in every morning because it saves time. I work in the car dictating letters and so forth. I drive myself most of the time though, Meech has got a cushy job and he knows it. But don't think I forget old friends. I tell you what, you and your wife must come out and have dinner one night. And we'll use the Rolls.'

Harold protested, but a few days later a letter came, signed 'Blanche Cutler', saying that Jack was delighted that an old friendship had been renewed, and suggesting a dinner date. Phyllis could hardly contain her pleasure, and was both astonished and furious when Harold said they shouldn't go, they would be like poor relations.

'What are you talking about? He's your old friend, isn't he? And he's been decent to you, offering you a job. If *he's* not snobby, I don't see why you should be.'

'I told you I don't like him. We're not friends.'

She glared at him. 'You're jealous, that's all. You're a

failure yourself, and you can't bear anybody to be a success.'

In the end of course they went.

Cutler and Harold left the office in the Rolls, driven by Meech, who was in his middle twenties, and they collected Phyllis on the way. She had bought a dress for the occasion, and Harold could see that she was taking everything in greedily, the way Meech sprang out to open the door, the luxurious interior of the Rolls, the cocktail cabinet from which Cutler poured drinks, the silent smoothness with which they travelled. Cutler paid what Harold thought were ridiculous compliments on Phyllis's dress and appearance, saying that Harold had kept his beautiful young wife a secret.

'You're a lucky man, my old boiler.'

'Harold said that was what you called him. It seems a silly name.'

'Just a reminder of schooldays,' Cutler said easily, and Harold hated him.

The Cutlers lived in a big red brick house in the outer suburbs, with a garden of more than an acre and a swimming pool. Blanche was a fine, imposing woman, with a nose that seemed permanently raised in the air. Another couple came to dinner, the man big and loud-voiced like Cutler, his wife a small woman loaded down with what were presumably real pearls and diamonds. The man was some sort of stockbroker, and there was a good deal of conversation about the state of the market. Dinner was served by a maid in cap and apron, and was full of foods covered with rich sauces which Harold knew would play havoc with his digestion. There was a lot of wine, and he saw with dismay that Phyllis's glass was being refilled frequently.

'You and Jack were great friends at school, he tells me,' Blanche Cutler said, nose in the air. What could Harold do but agree? 'He says that now you are his right hand man. I do think it is so nice when old friendships are continued in later life.'

He muttered something, and then was horrified to hear the word *boiler* spoken by Phyllis.

'What's that?' the stockbroker asked, cupping hand to ear. Phyllis giggled. She was a little drunk.

'Do you know what they used to call Harold at school? A boiler. What does it mean, Jack, you must tell us what it means.'

'It was just a nickname.' Cutler seemed embarrassed. 'Because his name was Boyle, you see.'

'I know you're hiding something from me.' Phyllis tapped Cutler flirtatiously on the arm. 'Was it because he looks like a tough old boiling fowl, very tasteless? Because he does. I think it's a very good name for him, a boiler.'

Blanche elevated her nose a little higher, and said that they would have coffee in the drawing room.

Meech drove them home in the Rolls, and gave Phyllis his arm when they got out. She clung to it, swaying a little as they moved towards the front door. Indoors, she collapsed on the sofa and said, 'What a lovely, lovely evening.'

'I'm glad you enjoyed it.'

'I liked Jack. Your friend Jack. He's such good company.'

'He's not my friend, he's my employer.'

'Such an attractive man, very sexy.'

He remembered the salesman. 'I thought you only liked younger men. Cutler's older than I am.'

She looked at him with a slightly glazed eye. 'Dance with me.'

'We haven't got any music.'

'Come *on*, doesn't matter.' She pulled him to his feet and they stumbled through a few steps.

'You're drunk.' He half-pushed her away and she fell to

the floor. She lay there staring up at him.

'You bastard, you pushed me over.'

'I'm sorry, Phyl. Come to bed.'

'You know what you are? You're a boiler. It's a good name for you.'

'Phyl. Please.'

'I married a boiler,' she said, and passed out. He had to carry her up to bed.

In the morning she did not get up as usual to make his breakfast, in the evening she said sullenly that there was no point in talking any more. Harold was just a clerk and would never be anything else, didn't want to be anything else.

On the day after the party Cutler came into Harold's office in the afternoon, and said he hoped they had both enjoyed the evening. For once he was not at ease, and at last came out with what seemed to be on his mind.

'I'm glad we got together again, for old times' sake. But look here, I'm afraid Phyl got hold of the wrong end of the stick. About that nickname.'

'Boiler.'

'Yes. Of course it was only meant affectionately. Just a play on your name.' Did Cutler really believe that, could he possibly believe it? His red shining face looked earnest enough. 'But people can get the wrong impression as Phyl did. Better drop it. So, no more boiler. From now on, it's Jack and Harold, agreed?'

He said that he agreed. Cutler clapped him on the shoulder, and said that he was late for an appointment on the golf course. He winked as he said that you could do a lot of business between the first and the eighteenth holes. Five minutes later Harold saw him driving away at the wheel of the Rolls, a cigar in his mouth.

In the next days Cutler was away from the office a good deal, and came into Harold's room rarely. At home Phyllis spoke to him only when she could not avoid it. At night they lay like statues side by side. He reflected that, although they had more money, it had not made them happier.

Ten days after the dinner party it happened.

Harold went that day to the vegetarian restaurant across the park. Something in his nut steak must have disagreed with him, however, because by mid-afternoon he was racked by violent stomach pains. He bore them for half an hour and then decided that he must go home.

The bus took him to the High Road, near his street. He turned the corner into it, walked a few steps and then stopped, unbelieving.

His house was a hundred yards down the street. And there, drawn up outside it, was Cutler's gold and silver Rolls.

He could not have said how long he stood there staring, as though by looking he might make the car disappear. Then he turned away, walked to the Post Office in the High Road, entered a telephone box and dialled his own number.

The telephone rang and rang. On the wooden framework of the box somebody had written 'Peter loves Vi'. He rubbed a finger over the words, trying to erase them.

At last Phyllis answered. She sounded breathless.

'You've been a long time.'

'I was in the garden hanging out washing, didn't hear you. You sound funny. What's the matter?'

He said that he felt ill and was coming home, was leaving the office now.

She said sharply, 'But you're in a call box, I heard the pips.'

He explained that he had suddenly felt faint, and had been near a pay telephone in the entrance hall.

'So you'll be back in half an hour.' He detected relief in her voice.

During that half hour he walked about, he could not afterwards have said in what streets, except that he could not bear to approach his own. He could not have borne to see Cutler driving away, a satisfied leer on his face at having once again shown the boiler who was master. Through his head there rang, over and over, Phyllis's words *such an attractive man, very sexy*, words that now seemed repeated in the sound of his own footsteps. When he got home Phyllis exclaimed at sight of him, and said that he did look ill. She asked what he had eaten at lunch, and said that he had better lie down.

In the bedroom he caught the lingering aroma of cigar smoke, even though the window was open. He vomited in the lavatory and then said to Phyllis that he would stay in the spare room. She made no objection. During the evening she was unusually solicitous, coming up three times to ask whether there was something he would like, taking his temperature and putting a hand on his forehead. The touch was loathsome to him.

He stayed in the spare room. In the morning he dressed and shaved, but ate no breakfast. She expressed concern.

'You look pale. If you feel ill come home, but don't forget to call first just in case I might be out.'

So, he thought, Cutler was coming again that day. The pearl handled revolver, small as a toy, nestled in his pocket when he left. He had never fired it.

He spent the morning looking out of his window, but Cutler did not appear. He arrived soon after lunch, brought by Meech as usual. He did not come to Harold's office.

Half an hour passed. Harold took out the revolver and balanced it in his hand. Would it fire properly, would he be able to shoot straight? He felt calm but his hand trembled.

He took the lift up to the top floor, and opened the door of Cutler's office without knocking. Cutler was talking to a recording machine, which he switched off.

'Why the hell don't you knock?' Then he said more genially, 'Oh, it's you, my old – Harold. What can I do for you?'

Harold took out the little revolver. Cutler looked astonished, but not frightened. He asked what Harold thought he was doing.

Harold did not reply. Across the desk the boiler faced the man who had ruined his life. The revolver went crack crack. Blue smoke curled up from it. Cutler continued to stare at him in astonishment, and Harold thought that he had failed in this as he had failed in so many things, that even from a few feet he had missed. Then he saw the red spot in the middle of Cutler's forehead, and the big man collapsed face down on his desk.

Harold walked out of the room, took the lift and left the building. He did not reply to the doorman, who asked whether he was feeling all right, he looked rather queer. He was going to give himself up to the police, but before doing so he must speak to Phyllis. He did not know just what he wanted to say, but it was necessary to show her that he was not a boiler, that Cutler had not triumphed in the end.

The bus dropped him in the High Road. He reached the corner of his street.

The gold and silver Rolls was there, standing outside his house.

He walked down the street towards it, feeling the terror of a man in a nightmare. Was Cutler immortal, that he should be able to get up from the desk and drive down here? Had he imagined the red spot, had his shots gone astray? He knew only that he must find out the truth.

When he reached the car it was locked and empty. He

opened his front door. The house was silent.

The house was silent and he was silent, as he moved up the stairs delicately on tiptoe. He opened the door of the bedroom.

Phyllis was in bed. With her was the young chauffeur Meech. A cigar, one of his master's cigars, was stubbed out in an ashtray.

Harold stared at them for a long moment of agony. Then, as they started up, he said words incomprehensible to them, words from the ritual of school. 'A boiler fails in everything he does. I am a boiler.'

He shut the door, went into the bathroom, took out the revolver and placed the tiny muzzle in his mouth. Then he pulled the trigger.

In this final action the boiler succeeded at last.

The Murderer

Howard Carey had always been what he thought of as fastidious, and his wife Ellen once called downright prudish, in sexual matters, and at first he did not understand what the woman was saying to him.

He glanced at his watch, under the vague impression that she had said something about the time. Then she repeated the suggestion in words that were unmistakable. He recoiled slightly, shook his head and walked on, but she moved on with him using obscenities, murmuring things that appalled him. He turned on her, ready to threaten her with the police, and saw under the street lamp that this was not a woman but a young girl. She wore a white mackintosh, had hair that under the light seemed a remarkable shade of reddish gold, and her features were delicate and pale. She could not be more than sixteen, was perhaps less. He would have liked to say to her that she should be at home, that she might contract a disease, half a dozen other things. In fact he only quickened his step and hurried away from her. 'Too old for it, are you?' she shouted after him.

The encounter worried and upset him. This was suburban London, not the centre of town where he knew that such things went on. They were no more than a couple of minutes from the Underground station, and less than ten minutes' walk from his home. He had read in the local paper about prostitution and mugging, and about drivers who crawled along beside the kerb trying to pick up women, but had never truly believed in such things. How could any woman bring herself to say such things as the girl had suggested to him? He arrived home in a state of shock.

The house was called Mon Repos. It was one in a short road of exactly similar houses, all of which had names, names which included Eagle's Nest, Chez Nous, Everest and Happy Landings. The houses had been built between the wars. They were red brick semi-detached, with bow windows in the front covered by lace or net curtains. Variety was provided by the doors, which were in different colours, as well as by the house names. A few bold spirits had replaced the wooden doors by glass ones with a design engraved on them. The Dempseys next door at Happy Landings had a glass door which showed mermaids rising from the waves. Howard and Ellen had discussed it at length. Ellen liked the design, but Howard thought that it was vulgar.

Once indoors he felt a little better. It was reassuring to see the three-piece suite, with both chairs and sofa facing the television set, the nest of tables that were pulled out when friends came in for coffee, the prints of local scenes on the walls, the photograph of Rod and Jean. Rod had been living in Canada for two years now, and was doing very well in his job as some kind of engineer. There was more space, he said, more opportunity, you had a better life altogether. Perhaps he was right, perhaps they would go out and pay the visit they had often talked about.

He looked at his watch. Ellen might be home soon, or she might be another hour or two. She had worked for several years as secretary in a firm of solicitors and her chief, Mr McIntyre, asked her to work late a couple of evenings a week. Howard himself, knowing this, had done some little jobs at the insurance firm where he was deputy sub-controller of the small Complaints Section. It had always been a source of gratification to Howard that they both worked in such sound occupations. He would not have liked it if Ellen had been employed in something rather doubtful, like an art gallery.

He went upstairs to wash his hands – that was how he thought of it, for he did not like to name his bodily necessities – and looked in the bathroom glass. It showed a lean face with thinning grey hair, lines on either side of the narrow nose, deep-set grey-blue eyes, a thin mouth. The expression was anxious, as though he were expecting something unpleasant to happen.

'Too old for it, are you?' He was fifty-three, Ellen six years younger. They had married young, because Rod was on the way. The birth had been difficult. After it Ellen had not seemed to welcome his attentions for a while, and then – well, it had not been easy to make ends meet on his salary, and if he were frank he would have to say that it had always been in his mind that an unintended successor to Rod would be a disaster. And then they had both been immensely occupied with Rod, with finding the money to send him to a good private day school and to University, so that it had seemed nothing else much mattered. Of course things had been easier financially after Ellen took a typing course and got a job.

He became aware that he was still staring into the glass. In it he seemed to see a different world from the one in which Ellen and he played bridge sometimes with neighbours and went occasionally to local whist drives or socials, in which he mowed the small lawn at the back once a week from spring to autumn, wound the grandfather clock in the hall every Sunday night, and never used any word with a sexual connotation or a swear word of any kind. In that other world people spoke as the young girl with reddish gold hair had spoken to him, used every possible word and committed every possible action, first making themselves insensible by drugs or drink to the very idea of right or wrong. In the other world they would sneer at everything that was right, reasonable and respectable. He had a sudden vision of the girl standing in their living room with others of her kind and doing dirty things everywhere, not just breaking things up but making an actual trail of filth all around. . .

He closed his eyes and the vision became more vivid, opened them again and it had disappeared, leaving his own face looking anxiously into the glass. He went down to the kitchen and got himself biscuits and cheese. Ellen cooked in the evenings, but when she worked late he ate a hot lunch and had something light for supper. They never took food into the living room for fear of leaving crumbs, and he ate at the kitchen table while he read the evening paper. The front page story was about a pop star who was leaving England because taxes were too high. He was shown smiling, about to board a plane, with a girl on either arm. In the story below the picture he said that they were two of his harem. Inside the paper there was a full page story about a schoolgirl who had killed herself because several others had been bullying her, forcing the girl to steal from her parents under threat of being tortured.

Howard went into the living room and turned on the TV. He enjoyed sports programmes, a family drama, or anything historical, but tonight there seemed to be nothing but what were called thrillers, with people being hit on the head or shot. He watched one of them to pass the time, but did not care for it. At nine o'clock it occurred to him that Ellen was later than usual. Perhaps Mr McIntyre had taken her to supper, which had happened occasionally when there was a lot of work to be done.

The bell rang just after ten o'clock. A policeman stood there, with sergeant's stripes on his arm.

'Mr Carey? May I come in?'

'What is it?' His thoughts moved at once, for some reason, to the girl in the white mackintosh.

'Your wife is Mrs Ellen Carey? I am afraid I have some

bad news. Best to sit down.'

Howard sat in one of the armchairs, looking up at the sergeant, who had a dark blue chin in need of a shave.

'Do you know a Mr John McIntyre?'

'I have never met him, but yes, he is my wife's employer.'

'Your wife was a passenger in Mr McIntyre's car tonight when it was involved in an accident.'

'Ellen's been hurt? She's in hospital?'

'I said the news was bad, sir. The car came out of a side road and was hit broadside on by a lorry. We haven't got all the details of just how it happened. The lorry driver is in hospital with concussion.'

'And Ellen?'

'I'm sorry, sir. Both car passengers were killed outright.'

Everybody was tremendously kind. Sergeant Stubbs (that was his name) had talked to Bill and Carol Dempsey at Happy Landings next door, and Howard spent the night there, and the next couple of days as well. Ellen's elder sister Norah, whom Howard had never much liked, came up from the country and stayed nearly a week. At the office the manager, Mr Langport, had called him and had a long chat, which ended with the suggestion that Howard should take some time off.

'Go away somewhere, stay with relatives.'

'I have no close relatives except my son in Canada. Otherwise only cousins.'

'What about staying with one of them?'

Howard shook his head. 'We haven't been in touch for years.'

'Your wife's relatives then?'

'No, I don't think that would do.' The thought of staying with Norah was not to be contemplated. 'I think the best thing is to go on working.'

'Very well. But if you change your mind and decide you'd like a few days off, just say the word.'

Yes, kindness everywhere. And nobody kinder than Rod, who flew over for the inquest. Jean stayed behind because she was expecting. Rod had filled out since he left England, and now seemed twice the size of his father. He stood in front of the gas fire in the living room and asked: 'What are you going to do, dad?'

'Do? I don't know what you mean.'

'What I mean is —' Rod gave it up and began again. 'Why not come back with me? Jean would love to see you, and there's plenty of room.'

No doubt that was so. He had seen photographs of Rod's home, which was said to be a ranch style house whatever that was, and it certainly looked much bigger than Mon Repos. He stayed silent while Rod elaborated the theme.

'Even the old skinflint where you work has said you ought to get away. If you come back with me you can look round and see how you like it. Then if you did, you could put this little place on the market —'

'You mean stay there, go to live in Canada? Give up my position in the firm?'

'Oh come on, dad, you know you're just a dogsbody. I mean, that's why mum went to work, isn't it?' He went on hurriedly. 'I know, it was to pay for my education and all that. Maybe the firm has a branch out there and could transfer you. Or if they didn't, no need to worry, you could stay with us as long as you liked while you found a job.'

Howard said stiffly, 'Thank you, Rod. I appreciate the offer, but I couldn't possibly leave this house.'

'Mon Repos? This stuffy little place? But dad, don't you see things will be different for you now mum's gone? At least move out into a flat, something easier to manage —'

'That's enough, Rod. I'm sure you mean well, but I

shouldn't think of moving from here. It may be a stuffy little place, but it is where you were brought up.'

That was the end of the discussion. After a week Rod flew back, and to his surprise Howard found that he was not sorry to see his son go. He wanted, more than anything, time to reflect and to be alone.

At the inquest what happened had been explained. The car had come out of a side turning on a curve and the driver's view of the road, which would have been poor anyway, had been obscured by a parked car. The lorry driver had probably been travelling faster than he should have been, but he could not have seen the car until it was too late to brake.

There was only one puzzling thing. The office was in the City, and the accident had taken place some miles away, in St John's Wood. The point did not concern the coroner and was not mentioned at the inquest, but it worried Howard because he could not understand it. Ellen had said that if Mr McIntyre took her out to eat, it was always somewhere near the office.

There seemed to be a conspiracy to prevent him from being alone. The Dempseys asked him in to supper once or twice a week and regularly for Sunday lunch, other neighbours dropped in for a chat, the vicar came round and so did a member of the committee that ran the church socials, to ask if he could lend a hand with the next outing. His chief Hebden, the sub-controller, with whom he had never been particularly friendly, surprised Howard by asking him to dinner. He accepted on the spur of the moment, but the evening was not a success. Hebden and he had little in common, and Mrs Hebden kept referring to what she called his tragic loss, and said that she thought lorries should not be allowed on the same roads as cars. Howard left, determined not to accept another invitation.

He had to show determination in getting free of the

Dempseys. Carol had taken to coming round almost every evening, bringing hot soup or a piece of jam tart. When she offered to sort through Ellen's clothes and give them to some good cause she favoured, he said that he would do it himself.

'But Howard, that's foolish.' The Dempseys were a little older than the Careys, but Carol dressed and acted younger than her years. She was a dumpy little woman who always wore bright clothes, which he disliked. 'I mean, you're just making things more painful for yourself.'

The clothes, Howard decided, were not the only things he disliked about Carol. She had a slightly lop-sided nose that he found distasteful. 'It's very kind of you, but I can do them.'

'At least let me help. Two do these things so much more easily than one. I shouldn't pry into anything.'

He found suddenly that his whole body was shaking. 'What do you mean? What would there be to pry into, as you call it?'

'Nothing, Howard. I didn't mean —'

'Why do you want to stick your nose into our affairs?' As he spoke the nose, with its small but decisive turn near the end, looked enormously enlarged and seemed to quiver with a life of its own.

'If that's your attitude I won't mention it again.'

'And I don't want this stuff.'

Howard went to give back the bowl of fruit jelly she had brought in, but it slipped from his hands and fell to the floor, breaking the bowl. Carol said nothing, but walked out of the kitchen. Later he bought a replacement bowl and put it outside their back door. After that there were no more invitations to dinner, and no little dishes were brought in.

Nevertheless, Carol had been right in saying that he

must do something about Ellen's things. He threw into the dustbin the pots of cosmetics, scent and other things on her dressing table – she must have spent a lot of money on such stuff – but her dresses hung in the cupboard, her other clothes were in a chest of drawers. He packed a suitcase full of them, and took it down to the local Oxfam shop in the little Morris car they had had for years. That's that, he thought as he returned, and it's been done without any help from that sly-nosed bitch next door.

He was surprised to find himself thinking so coarsely.

On the next evening he found the letters.

There was one drawer in the chest that Ellen had always kept locked. It was her personal drawer, she said, and when he asked what she meant by that, she laughed and said that curiosity killed the cat. The key had been in her bag at the time of the accident, and was returned to him after the inquest. When he turned it in the lock he expected to find little more than Ellen's jewellery, which she had told him she kept there.

The jewellery was there, the few inexpensive bits he had been able to afford and other things too, a diamond ring, a pair of pearl earrings, what looked like a ruby necklace. He had never seen them before. Had they belonged to Ellen's mother? The box containing the ring looked modern. There were other things that occasioned him no surprise, a photograph taken on their wedding day and pictures of Rod at school.

And there were the letters.

There were more than twenty of them, in their envelopes, addressed to Mrs Howard Carey. He remembered one of them arriving. Ellen had said it was from an old school friend, and he had said that she wrote a good firm hand. He had said nothing further, and he would never have thought of looking at her correspondence. But these letters were from no old school friend. They began 'Dearest Ellen' or 'Darling', and were signed 'Mac'. They told the story of a love affair. The first letter had been written several years ago, the last was less than three months old.

Howard Carey was a methodical man. He sat down on the bed with the letters and read them in chronological order, so that he had the whole story. Mac of course was Mr McIntyre, and it seemed that they had become lovers soon after she went to work for him. He was married, but his wife was hopelessly neurotic, in and out of mental institutions. The letters had been written when McIntyre had taken his wife away on holiday during short periods of recovery, and so had not seen Ellen for two or three weeks. The wife's illness made any thought of marriage impossible, but those evenings when she had been 'working late' had been spent in his St John's Wood apartment. There were references to 'the agony of parting' and 'sending you back to that crusty dry old stick who thinks of you only as his housekeeper'. And there were other remarks about Howard. 'I cannot bear to think of you in his arms, but then from what you say he never holds you in them. . . You say that if you left him it would break his heart, but what makes you think he has one? He has never cared for you, does not know what love means'. Then there were passages about 'burning for you' and 'longing for you,' as well as explicit words and phrases about making love, words that reminded him of what had been said by the young girl in the street.

He took two of the pills prescribed for him by the doctor, but could not sleep. What had Ellen been like? He switched on the light and looked long and earnestly at the photograph beside the bed, trying to discover in the features of the woman he had known the slut who had entered McIntyre's bed. She was in her forties. Did women have the desires mentioned in the letters at such an age?

When he turned off the light again, sexual images rioted through his mind, he saw Ellen happily shrieking obscenities. Then he must have slept, because she appeared with extraordinary vividness before him, laughing and saying: 'Of course I do it, I do it with anybody–*except you*.' He woke crying out, and did not sleep again.

It was from this evening onwards that Howard Carey felt he really understood the meaning of the world around him, and knew the purpose of his life. He did his work in the Complaints Department with reasonable efficiency, although Hebden told Mr Langport that Carey hardly seemed to be there half the time and in his opinion should be compelled to take some leave. The manager called Carey in for a chat, but saw nothing wrong. When he asked how things were going Carey said very well, he was much clearer in his mind now. It was a slightly odd answer, but hardly justified sending a man on leave.

So Howard went on working, arriving and leaving punctually. He shopped at the local supermarket, mostly foods that could be heated quickly. He washed up after eating, and then used the vacuum cleaner, so that Mon Repos was scrupulously clean. After eating, washing up and cleaning the house, he went for a long walk in the winter night. If while out walking he saw neighbours, like the Dempseys, he ignored them. His walk usually ended at one or other local pub, where he drank half a pint of beer and looked keenly at the women who came in unaccompanied. One evening a man told him that if he was looking for a bit of stuff, he'd find plenty at the Rising Sun. After that his walks ended there, but he did not find what he was looking for. He was accosted outside the pub a couple of times, but brusquely rejected the invitations made to him. Every night, after his return, he read the letters. He now knew several parts of them by heart.

He saw the knife on a night when the pavements and road gleamed with rain, a slanting rain that he trudged through with hat pulled down over his eyes. The knife was in the window of a seedy little shop, among shears, scissors and nail clippers. It had a long thin blade narrowing to a point, so that it resembled a miniature sword, and it seemed to Howard that it glittered like a jewel among all the rubbish beside it. Beneath it was a label: *Stiletto type blade, many uses.*

The shop was closed when he came home in the evening, but he bought the knife at the weekend.

'Very nice little job, sir,' the man behind the counter said appreciatively. 'Beautiful cutting edge. Clicks back into the handle too. On a spring.' He demostrated.

Howard held it with the point on his palm, moved it fractionally downwards. A bead of blood showed.

'You have to be careful of that point, sir. I'll get you something.'

'It doesn't matter.' Howard dabbed with a handkerchief. 'I'll take it.'

When he returned from this expedition the Dempseys were at their gate. He was passing them with a nod when Carol spoke.

'Horrible weather. Don't know when the winter's going to end. And you have to be out in it such a lot, don't you? We've seen you coming home once or twice.'

They had been spying on him! He did not reply, simply glared. But she went on.

'Why not come in tomorrow for Sunday lunch? So long since we've seen you.'

He muttered that he was too busy, had no time, and slammed his gate, leaving them staring after him.

After that he took the car out at nights and became one of the kerb crawlers. He had seen their technique in his walks. They moved along, hardly ever at more than five miles an hour, stopping when they saw one or two girls together, sometimes flashing their lights. There would be a brief discussion. Then the girls might move away or one – occasionally both – would get into the car, which speeded up as it drove away.

Now he did this himself. Girls came up and spoke to him, offering various 'services' as they called it, none of which he accepted. After a few days he became known, and some of the rejected girls were annoyed. One abused him at the car window.

'What do yer bleedin' want, then? Know what you are, just a dirty old man wants to hear girls talk about it and that's all. You keep out of my way or I'll tell my feller. He'll do you over, I can tell you that.'

After that he moved to another area a few streets away, one which he had avoided because it contained so many blacks, and he was a little afraid of them. Sure enough, one night a black girl opened the car door and sat down beside him. A black man came to the window grinning, and said, 'You want little Joanna?'

'No. I didn't ask her to get in, I don't want her.'

'That ain't what he said, is it Joanna? You hurt my little girl's feelings, I don't like that, you better give her a fiver, show you don't mean it.'

'I'll call the police.'

The man came round to Howard's door, opened it, stuck his head inside and said, 'You won't call pussy.'

The knife was in his pocket, but he dared not draw it. He gave the girl the money and drove away, pursued by raucous laughter.

In the end he found her by chance, in a street remote from the areas of prostitution. He was driving down it when he saw ahead of him the white mackintosh and the reddish gold hair. He pulled up beside her and opened the passenger door.

'Get in.'

She looked doubtfully at him, then said 'No, thank you.'

Of course she was nervous, it was off her beat. He leant over, pulled her arm, jerked her into the car and closed the door in one motion, drove off.

'What the hell are you doing?' she said.

He spoke rapidly. 'Look, we met before and I said no then but I didn't mean it, everybody wants it, my wife did, she loved it. She liked to be held in his arms naked and why not?' His right hand was in his pocket, he had the knife out and open.

'I don't know what you're talking about. Just let me out.'

'This is what everybody wants,' he said. He leaned over and put in the knife. 'Ellen,' he said, 'Hold me, Ellen.'

She did not cry out, so he withdrew the knife and plunged it in again. Now she leaned over and, with a sigh, came to rest in his arms. He pulled up, and put an arm round her. They were under a street lamp and only now, as the blood from her white mackintosh stained his hand and the light showed her features clearly, a rather coarse face with a twisted nose strangely like Carol Dempsey's, did he realise that he had picked up the wrong girl.

A Theme for Hyacinth

Happiness, Robin Edgley thought as he felt the sun on his chest and stomach and legs, seeping through the epidermis to irradiate the blood and sinew and, yes, heart beneath; it is by pure chance that I have discovered happiness for the first time in my life. If Felix had not been laid low by influenza and been delayed leaving England for a week, Gerda would never have spoken to me and this would have been simply another holiday. Instead, it was a revelation to himself of his inmost nature.

Happiness, happiness! It was a golden body that you held in your hands on a green island beside a blue sea, but it was also – to move beyond that rather seaside-posterish conception – the inward reassurance given by his love for Gerda, the feeling of merging his identity with that of another human being, something that went beyond the possibilities of words.

Pleasurable warmth was turning into heat. Perhaps his front had been cooked sufficiently. He removed the bandage from his eyes, glanced round, and saw that he shared the terrace beside the sea with half a dozen old men and women; he turned onto his stomach and picked up the poetry anthology he had been reading. One poem, *Le Monocle de Mon Oncle* by Wallace Stevens, fascinated him. It was a middle-aged man's reflections on love:

> In the high west there burns a furious star.
> It is for fiery boys that star was set
> And for sweet-smelling virgins close to them.
> The measure of the intensity of love
> Is measure, also, of the verve of earth.

True, he thought. He felt in himself a sharpening of the

senses, a deepened awareness of everything about him. But the next verse provoked disagreement.

When amorists grow bald, then armours shrink
Into the compass and curriculum
Of introspective exiles lecturing.
It is a theme for Hyacinth alone.

No, no, he cried silently. His head was silvered and not bald, but the point was that love between a mature man and a young woman could contain everything felt by those 'fiery boys' – and more, much more. Was the poem not proved untrue by almost the first words Gerda had spoken to him?

He was wondering at that time, three days ago, why he had ever come. He had succumbed to the boyish eagerness of his cousin Felix, and had regretted it almost immediately. Looking sideways at him out of those dark eyes that were absurdly long-lashed for a man's, Felix had said he was going away and asked why Nunky – which was his name for Robin, although they were not blood relations – didn't come too.

'I'm fed up with bloody agents, bloody producers, bloody theatre. Getting out of it, Nunky, going to look for the sun. Let them bloody ring my flat and not find me, they'll be keener when I come back. Since you're a man of leisure, why not make it a twosome?' Where was he going? He didn't know but it turned out to be Yugoslavia, the Adriatic coast, Dubrovnik. 'Boiling hot, wonderful swimming, fishing, and cheap. Not that that matters to you, but it does to me. And we might find a couple of birds. If you're so inclined.'

Again that sideways glance from the fine eyes that – he could admit it frankly now – always disturbed him. The disturbance came from the doubts about himself raised by such glances and by the impulse he felt at times to put an arm round the young man's shoulders, to push him playfully over onto a sofa when they had an argument. It was five years since Mary's death and he had neither remarried nor even engaged in a love affair since then. Was there something wrong with him?

Thinking of his own fastidiousness, of the care he took about the colour and fit of clothes, of his liking for picking up nice little pieces of bric-a-brac and of putting them in just the right spot in his flat, he wondered whether he could possibly be (a word he disliked using, disliked even the thought of) queer? Or was it just that the rackety life Felix lived fascinated him, shifting quarterly from flat to flat, often out of work and sometimes tremendously hard up? Occasionally Robin had lent him small sums of money which had always been returned, but he had worried even about these. Was he trying to buy affection?

He could admit all this now, since Gerda had proved that there was nothing queer about him.

So much for Felix, who had done him the best turn of his life by contracting influenza and by telephoning, in a woebegone voice about which there was as always a hint of self-mockery, to say that he would come out as soon as he felt better. But these had not been Robin's thoughts as he took a hot bath, changed into a dashing maroon dinner jacket, and sat down to dinner alone on that first night in the hotel. Afterward he stood on the terrace leaning on his silver-headed malacca cane, and stared gloomily at the lights of the old city. He felt a touch on his arm.

'You will forgive me if I speak to you,' the girl said. 'But I could not help looking at you in the restaurant. You were the most attractive man in the room.' She paused and made a careful amendment. 'That is not quite right. I should have said the most *interesting* man.'

That made it easier for him to say, 'Thank you.'

'My name is Gerda.'

'Robin Edgley.' She was young, blonde, beautiful. He

felt a moment's panic. 'Shall we sit down? Would you like a drink?'

When they were sitting in chairs that overlooked the bay, drinks by their sides, he felt a little more comfortable. 'You took my breath away. Do you often say that kind of thing to a strange man?'

'Never before. Please believe me.' She spoke gravely, and he did believe her. She was not, he now saw, quite the dazzling beauty he had thought. Her hair was silky and her features fine, but the large mouth turned down sulkily at the corners and her blue eyes were very wide apart under their thick blonde brows. The eyes looked cold, but a kind of warmth came from her, almost as if some fire burned within her. Her English was perfect, but accented.

He asked if she was German and she nodded. 'You're a very unusual girl.'

'Don't talk like that. As if you were my uncle.' She spoke sharply. 'We are the same age, you and I.'

'What nonsense. I might be your uncle. I am forty-five.' In fact, he was four years older.

'I did not mean in that way. We feel the same emotions. When you look at this landscape what do you feel?'

He looked into gathering darkness and she said impatiently, 'Not now. When you came.'

'Romantic, I suppose.'

'And subtle.'

'Yes, romantic in a subtle way,' he said, although he had not felt this at all.

'Young men do not feel such things. They bore me.' Without taking breath she asked, 'Shall we go for a walk?'

They walked in the Gradac Park, among old cypress and pine trees, above the sea. He found himself talking with unusual freedom, telling her that he had been a partner in a small firm manufacturing a new kind of air vent for kitchens, and that he had retired from it a couple of years ago. He tried to explain something of his feeling.

'Suddenly it seemed ridiculous, going in to an office every day. I thought, is this all I'm going to do with my life? Of course when Mary was alive it was different, but she died five years ago.'

'Mary?'

'My wife. I forgot you didn't know her. Isn't that silly?'

'Nothing about you is silly. Yes, there is one thing.' She pointed to the stick. 'Why use that? It is for lame men.'

'Ah, but you don't realize —' With a twist and a flourish he drew the sword from its sheath. 'If I am attacked.'

'I think it is foolish.' In her precise English it sounded very definite. 'What else have you found in life?'

'I don't know. Places – all the places I haven't seen. Poetry – I always liked reading poetry. Meeting people, not just English people.'

'Have you found what you hoped?'

'I don't know. Enough to be glad that I gave up business.'

But as he spoke it seemed to him that something was terribly missing. He asked what she did, and she laughed deep in her throat.

'You will see.' She would say nothing more. On the way back he was very conscious of her physical presence at his side. There was something animal, assured yet stealthy, about the movements of her body. Once he touched her arm and felt an almost irresistible desire to grip her shoulders and turn her to him. Then the moment was over and they were walking along again.

In the hotel lobby he was uncertain whether to suggest a drink in his room. Then that moment also passed. She said good night and was walking away, the golden hair like a cap at the back of her head.

On the following morning he woke in excellent spirits. He ate breakfast on the balcony outside his room and watched tourists going off in coaches to Mostar, the bay of Kotor, and on the Grand Tour of Montenegro. The holiday makers, mostly brawny Germans and unbecomingly sunburned English, stood about chatting until they were shepherded by energetic guides into the coaches. The voices of the guides rang out like those of schoolteachers gathering children to cross the road.

'Hurry, please. We are already five minutes late.'

There was something familiar about the precision of the tone even as it floated up to him, and he identified her in a blue and white sleeveless dress, with a dark-blue peaked cap on the side of her head. She looked up, saw him, touched her fingers to her lips, then jumped into the coach and was gone.

He was in the sun lounge when the travellers returned in the early evening. He assured himself that he was not waiting for her, but the thrill that went through his body at the sight of her golden hair under the peaked cap was something he had not felt for years.

She came up to him at once. Beads of moisture marked her upper lip. He asked if she wanted a drink. She shook her head. 'I am not presentable. Those coaches are hot. But in ten minutes I should like a large, *large* gin and tonic.'

He had it waiting for her in the bar.

'So you're a guide.'

'Only for a few days, with this one party. On Sunday my husband comes out. Then we shall be on holiday.' Her petulant mouth turned down. 'His name is Porter, so that I am Gerda Porter. It sounds ridiculous. He is a travel agent. I thought it would be amusing to play the part of a guide, for just one party, so he arranged it.'

'He sounds nice.'

'Don't let us talk about him. Shall I come to your room now or after dinner?' He stared at her. 'I have shocked you? You do not like women to be frank?'

He went on staring and she looked back with one thick eyebrow raised, half smiling. 'Now,' he said and then added, with what he felt at the time to be wretched pusillanimity, 'in separate lifts. We must be careful.'

They went up in separate lifts. They did not come down to dinner.

Two days later her party went home. He watched her with them, talking to the men who asked about playing at the casino where only foreign currency was permitted and about making special trips to see what they called 'something of the way people really live here' (as though the Yugoslavs were another species), and with the women who engaged her in endless chats about what they could buy and what they could take home.

She handled all their queries with efficiency, courtesy and an apparently endless patience. After seeing them off at the airport she came back and sat in a chair beside him.

'I'm glad that's over. What a boring lot!'

'You handled them perfectly.'

'Why not? I used to be a travel courier. I was enjoying it. But after meeting you —' She left the sentence unfinished. 'We have three days.'

'Three days?'

'Before my husband arrives.' Her eyes were like blue marbles.

That day they explored Dubrovnik, intoxicated by the pleasure of being in a city sacred to walkers. They wandered from side to side of the Placa looking in the windows of shops that all seemed to sell the same goods, priced head scarfs and rugs in the Gundulic Square market, ate unidentifiable fish at a little restaurant in Ul Siroka, made a circuit of the ramparts. After lunch they drank coffee on the terrace of the Gradska Kafana by the harbour. Then they hired a motorboat with surprising ease, and in the motorboat discovered the island.

The Dalmatian coast is full of islands, including Lokrum, less than half a mile from the walled city, which appears to be covered with pine woods but in fact contains a park filled with subtropical vegetation and twenty small coves for bathers. Lokrum is a 'trippers' haunt', but a little beyond it there are a dozen tiny islands, no more than a few hundred yards long, some almost pure rock, others covered by shrubs and dwarf trees, and with natural landing places.

It was one of these that they found, rowing in the last few yards and pulling up the boat into a tiny bay. They took off their clothes, swam naked in the clear blue water, then walked back a few yards from the beach and made love on the grass. The walls of Dubrovnik were visible less than a mile away, yet they were completely alone. This is unreal, he told himself; it has nothing to do with any life I have ever known. These thoughts were interrupted by Gerda.

'Look at me! I sweat like a pig.' There was moisture on her brow and on her body. 'Disgusting. Not like you – your body is dry.'

'Dry with old age.'

'Don't talk like that, it's stupid. My husband is an old man.'

'Gerda —'

'And I do not wish you to call me Gerda, it is the name he uses. I tell you my secret name – it is Hella. You call me Hel.'

'Hel, you have shown me heaven,' he said inanely. 'Does he look like me, your husband?'

She snorted with laughter. 'You'll see.' With her face half buried in grass she told him about her life. Her parents had escaped from East to West Germany, and she had gone from West Germany to England, where she worked as an *au pair* girl. She had no intention of remaining with the family, but she could not get a job without a labour permit. So she forged one and was engaged as a courier by Porter Travel Limited.

'And then you married the boss.' He said it lightly, to hide the fact that her calm talk of forgery had shocked him.

'Yes.'

'You say he is – my age. Did he attract you?'

'Yes, but that was not important. He found out that my permit was no good, so it was the only thing to do. When I see something must be done I do it.'

'You're ruthless.'

'When it is necessary. But if I had known what it would be like —' Again she did not finish the sentence, but stared at him with her brilliant marble eyes. Then she turned and ran down again to the sea. He got up and followed her.

It was on the island, the following day, that he told her he loved her. This was something he had not said to any woman, except to Mary in the early days of their marriage. She made no reply. 'But you don't love me, Hel, do you?'

'I am not sure. Anyway it does not matter. It is Friday. On Sunday afternoon my husband will arrive.'

'Felix too. I've had a cable.' He had told her about Felix.

'When he is here it will be all over.'

'I want to marry you.' He had not known that he was going to say these words, but as soon as they were uttered he knew them to be true. She remained silent. 'Did you hear me?'

'I heard you. It is impossible.'

'Why?'

'My husband is a Catholic. He would not divorce me.'

'If you left him we could live together.' He was astonished to hear himself suggest it.

'He would bring a law case, drag you through the Courts. Would you like that, respectable Robin? There is only one way we could be together.'

'How?'

'If he were dead.'

He had closed his eyes. Now he opened them. She had a towel wrapped round her, and she was leaning on one arm looking at him. He realized at once that she meant they should kill her husband in some way. He was not even surprised, for he understood by now the total ruthlessness of her character. But he was a conventional man, and conventional words accurately expressed his reaction. 'You must be mad.'

She made no reply, but began to dress. They went down to the boat in silence. Then she put her arms round him. 'I love you, Robin, but how can I permit myself to do so? What would be the use?'

'If you loved me you wouldn't talk like that.'

'I love like a German. If I want something I try to get it. If I cannot get it I do without and don't complain. You do not have the courage to help me, so we have till Sunday. We can enjoy that much.'

But Robin did not enjoy it, or not in the same way. The sensual grip she exerted on him was very powerful. He had always thought of himself as a less than average sensual man, for he had never experienced with Mary anything like the feelings that Gerda inspired in him. The intensity of his actions and reactions during lovemaking frightened him, just as in a different way he was frightened by the feeling that he existed as an instrument for her satisfaction. He told himself that he loved her, but did he feel anything more than a sexual itch? Lines from another poem came into his head:

> But at my back from time to time I hear
> The sound of horns and motors which shall bring
> Sweeney to Mrs Porter in the spring.

To think of himself as apeneck Sweeney, the image of mindless sensuality, distressed and worried him. But over-riding such feelings was the longing he felt for her that made another part of himself say, 'This is the first happiness you have had in your long dreary life. Are you going to throw it away?'

He held out until Sunday morning. On Saturday they went to the island but it was not a success, and on Sunday morning neither of them suggested a visit. When they found that two places were vacant on a coach expedition to Cilipi, a few miles away, to see the peasants come to church in local costume, they got in.

The scene as they approached was farcical. Dozens of coaches were drawn up along the roadside. They parked half a mile from the church square. When they reached it, the place was packed with camera-carrying tourists, taking shots of everything in sight. A few locals moved in and out of the throng, the women wearing white nunlike coifs, embroidered blouses, and long black skirts. Tourists snapped cameras within inches of their faces, asked them to hold still, climbed onto cars to get angled shots. A scrawny American with white knees showing below baggy shorts aimed his camera at a fezzed village elder who sat placidly smoking a long clay pipe.

'Excuse it, please.' The American pushed Robin and Gerda aside, dropped to one knee, then suddenly flung himself flat onto the ground and squinted up at the Cilipian who stared into the distance with imperturbable dignity. Robin looked at Gerda. They both burst out laughing, then walked out of the square and the village down a rough path that led through scrub to nowhere.

'You do not have your cane.' He had left it in his room ever since that first evening. He said curtly she had been right, he did not need it. She glanced at him, said nothing.

'Did you ever see anything so awful as those tourists? The Yugoslavs must think we're all barbarians.'

'But I am a barbarian. You think so.' Her words were like an accusation.

She leaned against a rock. 'You are afraid of everything. If I said to you take me into that field, make love to me, would you do it?'

'Hel, it wouldn't be —' Two coiffed women came up the stony path. *'Dobar dan?'* he said.

'Dobar dan.' They passed on.

She said ironically, as he stumbled on a rock, 'You need your cane. I think you should carry it.' She wore dark glasses, but he knew that behind them her blue eyes would be cold. He could not bear the thought of losing her. 'Hel, tell me what you want.'

'It must be what *we* want.'

'What we want.' When he put his hand on her arm it seemed to burn him.

She told him in her precise English, speaking in a rapid low voice. She used sleeping tablets and would put two of them into her husband's coffee one day after lunch. Robin would take him out in the boat. In half an hour her husband would be asleep. Near the island the boat would overturn and the sleeping man would drown. Robin was a strong swimmer, he could easily reach the island. There he would wait until a boat saw him, or an expedition came looking for them from Dubrovnik.

'It would be murder.'

'He would know nothing.'

'I should be suspected. People have seen us together.'

'Do you think the Yugoslav police will trouble about that? They are peasants, like the people here. It is obviously an accident. Probably they do not find the body. And if they do —' The sulky mouth curved upward in a smile. 'I will tell you something. He cannot swim.'

'La Belle Dame sans Merci,' he said.

'What is that?'

'A poem. It means you are ruthless. And I am in thrall to you.'

'I do not understand.'

'Yes. It means that I say yes.'

She did not reply, did not take off the dark glasses, merely looked at him and nodded. Then she took his hand and led him into the field. The pleasure that followed was intense, and almost painful.

'You're looking uncommonly fit, Nunky,' Felix said. 'A fine bronzed figure of an Englishman. You bear every sign of not having missed me. Discovered any female talent?'

'Don't be absurd.'

'Most of them look over the age of consent to me.'

'I have been out once or twice with Mrs Porter. Her husband was on your plane. They're staying at this hotel.'

'Little fat chap – I remember meeting her. A blonde piece, a bit too Nordic for me.'

'She is of German origin,' he said with what he knew to be ridiculous stiffness.

Felix looked at him and whistled. 'You sound as if you've fallen for the fair Nordic lady. I shall have to look after you, Nunky, I can see that.'

He went out with Felix in the boat that afternoon, and landed on the island. They both swam and then Felix put on his skindiving equipment and disappeared for three-quarters of an hour while Robin lay on the beach and thought about Hel. Her absence ached in him like a tooth, and when Felix reappeared and talked enthusiastically about the marvellous clarity of the water so that he could see fish swimming fifty feet below him, and said it would be quite easy to swim from the island to Dubrovnik, he heard himself becoming unreasonably snappish.

The old relationship with Felix, in which he had responded eagerly to his young cousin's coquettish facetiousness, had been replaced by a feeling of irritation. He no longer wished to be called Nunky and felt no inclination to indulge in pseudoboyish horseplay. When the young man took out a mirror and began carefully to comb his hair he felt a faint stirring of distaste.

Closing his eyes he immediately saw Hel in bed with her fat stumpy husband, forced to accept his lovemaking or – worse still – welcoming it. He got up, walked to the water's edge, began to throw stones into the sea. Felix watched him with a smiling mouth and inquisitive eyes.

She introduced him to Porter that evening. Good heavens, Robin thought as he looked at the squat paunchy little man who shook hands with him, he's *old*! However did she bring herself to marry him? It was a shock to remember that Porter was no more than two or three years older than himself, but then there was the difference between them of a man who had kept his body in trim and one who had let it go to seed.

'Hear you've been squiring Gerda around, Mr Edgley. I appreciate that. Not that she's had much spare time, with this crazy idea she had of being guide to one of my parties. Had to indulge her – I'm an indulgent man, isn't that so, my dear?' He patted her hand.

'From what I saw she was a most efficient guide.'

'Should be. Used to do it for a living, now it's for fun. I tell you what I'd like, Robin – don't mind if I call you that, I know Gerda does – what I'd like is for you and your friend to be my guests this evening. Let's go and paint this little old Communist town red.'

'Norman knows all the best places,' Gerda said without smiling.

'I should, my dear, I should. The food at this place is – well, it's hotel food and that's all you can say for it. But I know a little place where – just you leave it to me.' He winked one eye.

It was a terrible evening. They ate a special Montenegrin dinner which began with smoked ham, followed by red mullet and *raznici,* which proved to be a brother to *kebab,* meat grilled on a skewer. The restaurant was set in a garden, just outside the city walls.

Porter – or as he insisted on being called, Norman – talked Serbo-Croat to waiters who responded in English. They drank slivovitz to begin with, continued with several bottles of full red Yugoslav wine, and ended with more slivovitz. Norman sent back one bottle of slivovitz with what sounded like a flow of objectionable remarks in Serbo-Croat. When the waiter shrugged and brought a bottle of another make he said triumphantly, 'You see. You have to know to get the right stuff.'

There was a band, and all three of them danced with Gerda. When Robin moved round, feeling the hard warmth of her body beneath his hand, he found the sensation almost intolerable. 'You see what he is like,' she said. 'An old man. Disgusting.'

'Not much older than I am.'

'Do not be stupid. It is not at all the same.'

'Hel, I have to see you, talk to you.'

'We cannot,' she said crisply. 'This I told you.'

'I just have to see you alone.'

'Impossible. Besides, what is there to talk about? Today is Sunday. Tomorrow after lunch.'

The dance was almost finished before he said, 'Yes.'

Felix danced with Gerda, holding her as lightly as possible, his arched nostrils slightly distended, his head held high in the manner of a horse ready to shy at what he may meet round the next corner. They seemed to exchange little conversation. Norman drank another glass of slivovitz, belched slightly.

'After this I want you to be my guests at the casino.'

'Very kind of you, but —' Robin protested.

'Won't take but for an answer. Beautiful, isn't she?'

An alarming remark. Robin did not know what to say. 'Very charming.'

'Some men would be jealous. Not me. I like it, like her to have other friends. I understand.' He drummed with his fingers on the table. Robin realized that his host was drunk. 'I've never regretted anything – want you to know that. No regrets, no heel taps. Loveliest girl I ever saw, married her. What d'you say to that?'

Robin had no desire to say anything to it. When Gerda and Felix came back, Porter rose a little unsteadily. 'May I have the pleasure?'

She said nothing, but moved into his arms. Felix seemed about to speak, then did not. Robin watched them dancing. Porter's arm was on her bare back, and he seemed to be talking continuously.

Felix, like a man who has come to a decision, said, 'Nunky.'

Irritation spilled over. 'Once and for all, will you please understand that I do not want to be called by that ridiculous name!'

'Sorry.'

There was a disturbance among the dancers. Gerda emerged from it, half supporting her husband. Porter sat down heavily, closed his eyes, and opened them again. He insisted they must all go on to the casino, but with the headwaiter's help they got a taxi and returned to the hotel. During the taxi ride Porter began to snore. At the hotel Felix and Robin each took an arm to get him into the lift. In the bedroom Gerda removed his jacket and waved them away.

'I can put him to bed, thank you. I have done it before.'

Alone in his room Robin looked at himself in the glass. Below the abundant white hair his face was youthful. Calves and thighs were slightly withered but his body was supple, his stomach flat.

'With this body I thee worship,' he said aloud. He picked up the malacca walking stick, drew the sword from it, made a few passes at an imaginary enemy. Perhaps he too was a little drunk, he thought, as he carried on a dialogue with himself while staring into the glass.

Robin Edgley, he said, retired director of a firm manufacturing fan ventilators, you are reaching out for happiness, and there is only one way to obtain it. Make up your mind to that. But what you are about to do is crazy, another part of himself said; you are thinking of forever but she is thinking of today and tomorrow and perhaps next year. And not only is it crazy but it is wrong, opposed to all the instincts you have lived by since youth. How can you imagine that after doing wrong you will be happy? What does that matter, the first voice said, when I have been given a glimpse of eternity. . .

It was a long time before he fell asleep, and when he slept he dreamed. He was in the sea and Porter was with him, the boat overturned; he was holding Porter under the water, but instead of submitting quietly the man flailed and twisted like a fish. Then Robin gripped a throat which was smooth, young, and white instead of the swollen wrinkled column he was expecting, and it was Hel's throat he was squeezing, her face that was gaspingly lifted to his own before he too started to gasp and thrash about, conscious that life was being pressed out of him . . .

He woke with the sheet twisted round his body. The dream disturbed him. There was some element in it that he could not recall; something had happened that his conscious mind refused to register. He looked at his watch and saw that it was only two o'clock. He did not sleep again until four. . .

In the morning Porter looked pale but cheerful. At eleven o'clock he was drinking a champagne cocktail on the terrace. 'Hear you put me to bed last night, old man, very nice of you. Sort of thing that's liable to happen, you know, first night.' He spoke like the victim of some natural disaster.

'How do you feel now?'

'I'm okay. Champagne with cognac always puts me right. Though mind you, it's got to be cognac, not this filthy local brandy. You're a fisherman, Gerda tells me.'

'I do fish, yes.'

'How about taking a boat after lunch, the two of us, eh?'

'I'm really not at all expert.'

'That's all right, neither am I. We'll just trawl for mullet and bream – what do they call 'em here, *dentex*? That's a hell of a name to give a fish.'

'What about your wife?'

'She wants to go to Lokrum, going to show it to that cousin of yours. I've been out half a dozen times myself, sooner do a bit of fishing. Bores Gerda, I know it does. Anyway, I want to have a quiet natter.'

'All right, let's go fishing.'

Later, walking round Dubrovnik with Felix, he learned a little more about the intended expedition to Lokrum. Sitting between the coupled columns in the elegant cloister of the Franciscan monastery, swinging a leg clad in tight sky-blue slacks, Felix calmly admitted that he had deliberately arranged it.

'Let's be frank about it, Porter's a slob but Hel's poison. You don't want to be mixed up with her.'

'I am not mixed up, as you put it.'

'Oh, come *on.*' Felix could not help posing, whatever his surroundings, and now he turned away from Robin so that his fine profile was outlined against the grey stone like the head on a coin. 'You follow her with your eyes wherever she goes, you treat her as though she were made of china. And believe me she's not, she's tough as old boots. I know her kind.' Robin made no reply. Felix went on. 'Even old slob Porter must spot it soon. So I thought I'd remove you from temptation this afternoon. And for the rest of the time we're here – well, they tell me there are lots of perfectly fascinating places to see on guided tours.'

'Thank you.' He knew how much Felix disliked guided tours.

'Think nothing of it. And now shall we go and look at the Museum of the Socialist Revolution? You know I've been longing to do that ever since I got here.'

They visited the museum and then went round the ramparts. Coming away from them down the narrow steps Felix slipped and fell. He got up and grimaced. He had twisted his ankle. After hobbling back to the hotel he borrowed Robin's stick. 'If I'm going to hobble I'll do it in style, look like a man of distinction.'

He was with Gerda alone for a few minutes before lunch. She wore an op art dress in zigzags that drew a great many eyes to her. Catching a brief glimpse of them both in a glass and admiring his own dark-blue linen shirt and pale trousers, he could not help thinking they made a handsome couple. She let him buy her a drink in the bar. She spoke rapidly.

'This afternoon your cousin takes me to Lokrum, so I shall be out of the way. You will drink coffee with us after lunch.'

'Hel, I don't know.'

'What?' she said sharply. 'What do you not know?'

'Whether I can go through with it.'

She finished her drink, turned on her heel, and left him.

After lunch it was Porter who stopped by their table and suggested that they all have coffee together. Really, Robin thought, if ever a man could be called the architect of his own destruction it was Porter – but no doubt Hel had put him up to it. She smiled briefly as she waited for them at the table, with coffee already poured. Porter was jovial.

'You know what made me marry Gerda? Because she's the most honest woman I ever met.'

'Is that so?' Felix made the question sound like an insult.

'You know she worked for me as a courier and I found she had a phony work permit. So when I said marry me she said, "I might consider it; this way at least I won't have to worry about a permit." '

'The kind of thing that other people think I am prepared to say.' Gerda spoke with a touch of complacency.

'And would you believe it, she made another condition. A girl in her position, making conditions with me!' He roared with laughter. ' "You're more than twice my age," she says, "you'll have the best years of my life. So what happens to me when you die?" She actually *said* that, mind you. So I told her I'd look after her, and I have.'

'Very rash.' Felix murmured the words so that Porter did not hear them, but Gerda did.

'I am a German, and Germans are realistic.' Her glance at Felix was hostile. It seemed likely to be an uncomfortable afternoon for them both on Lokrum. 'We will walk down to the boat with you. If you can manage that,' she said to Felix.

'I'm improving rapidly.' Certainly he limped much less as they went down to the harbour. Porter was carrying some fishing tackle in case, as he said, he had a chance to use it. Robin changed into clean shorts. The crisp elegance of his appearance contrasted favourably, he thought, with Porter's sweatstained shirt and general grubbiness.

The slick young man who rented the boat indicated with a slightly contemptuous air the trawling lines fixed to it, and Porter nodded and waved his hand to indicate that he did not need to be told. He climbed in, complete with fishing tackle. Robin in the stern started the outboard, and they were away. Felix and Gerda waved from the harbour.

They skirted Lokrum and moved into the open water beyond. Porter dropped his lines, lighted a pipe, and sat back. He looked what he was – a prosperous businessman carrying too much weight. Robin stared at him, unable to believe what he was going to do.

'Tell me something.' Porter's next words were inaudible. Robin almost closed the throttle, so that the boat jogged up and down on the blue water.

'What's that?'

'I like you, Robin, so I thought I ought to —' His next words were again inaudible. 'Gerda,' he ended.

'I can't hear properly.' He closed the throttle completely, so that the motor cut out. They drifted slowly toward the island, his island, only a few hundred yards away. Porter's voice came through he stillness.

'Gerda likes to be with me. I don't say she's happy, because she's not a contented person, never would be. But don't get the wrong idea.'

'I don't know what you mean.'

'She likes me. She thinks of crazy things, does them sometimes. Ran away from me once, came back after a couple of weeks, no money. She needs money, that's her motive power, like the engine that runs this boat. So she always comes back.'

'Why are you telling me this?' There was something wrong in the boat.

'Just wanted you to understand. I'm not a fool, Robin – I may look it but I'm not. Why do you think I let her do this crazy little job out here? Think I haven't got other couriers? I knew she wanted an affair, wanted to let off steam.'

With a feeling of disbelief he saw that his cane lay just below Porter's fishing tackle. 'How did that get there?' he cried.

'What? Oh, the cane. Your cousin asked me to slip it in with my tackle, thought you might need it. In case the rocks were slippery, he said. He's a bit of a joker, that boy.'

'I don't understand.'

'About Gerda now, don't get the wrong idea, that's all. You were just a pebble who happened to be on the beach. She doesn't like men of our age. I ought to know.' Porter knocked out his pipe. 'Okay, start her up again.'

Robin tugged savagely at the cord and the outboard sprang to life. They roared through the water with the throttle wide open. When will it happen, he thought, when are the pills going to work? I can't stand much more of this. He felt weary himself, a weariness that sprang from the bad dreams and restlessness of the night.

Porter's voice seemed to come from far away and he ignored it. The island loomed larger, and momentarily he lost his grip on the tiller. Porter was scrambling toward him, his face alarmed. The boat rocked. Robin began to laugh.

'Better not upset the boat when you can't swim,' Robin warned.

'Who the hell told you I couldn't swim? All fat men can swim. Here, give me the tiller, I'll take the boat in. Are you ill?'

He wanted to say that he had the situation under control and that Porter's own wife had said he was a non-swimmer; but suddenly he was too tired to speak. *She's* made a mess of it, he thought as Porter leaned over him, pushing him to the bottom of the boat in his anxiety to steer. *She put the pills in the wrong cup.* Then he could no longer keep his eyes open.

He was in the middle of a dream which was both pleasurable and disturbing. Pleasurable because he was not fighting for breath as he had been last night, nor involved in any kind of struggle. He lay on the island beach, just a few yards from the sea, the sun burning down. Concern about the boat was removed by the sight of it carefully drawn up onto the beach.

Good old Porter! All that nonsense about the boat overturning – it must have been nonsense because Porter could swim. It had been a figment of his imagintion. 'Figment,' he said happily, but could not hear the word. When he felt more energetic he would go into the sea.

Why was he disturbed then? Well, first of all, was he dreaming or not? 'Do I wake or sleep?' he asked, but again could hear no words spoken. But that was not the main thing. The main thing was that in his dream he had heard a cry. Perhaps the cry of a bird, but no bird was visible. Had the cry wakened him, or was he still dreaming?

He found it difficult to focus. The boat, like everything else, looked hazy. And now a monster appeared in the sea, vanished, reappeared briefly, then sank under the waves. What kind of monster? Dark and with nothing very distinguishable in the way of a head, a strange dark monster that writhed and splashed and vanished. The sea snake of Dubrovnik?

But surely sea snakes did not exist. I refuse to believe in you, monster, he thought, you are part of my dream. And sure enough the monster had gone – he *was* dreaming. He closed his eyes again.

When they reopened the sun was low in the sky and had lost its power. He felt cold, he knew that he was awake, and his uneasiness had increased. Where was Porter? Asleep somewhere else? It was still an effort to move, and a greater effort to think.

Had Porter gone back to Dubrovnik? There was something wrong with this idea, and he worked out what it was. Porter could not have gone to Dubrovnik or the boat would not still be on the beach.

Something else worried him, something done or said which he must try to remember. Was it perhaps that he had never even attempted what he had set out to do, that whether through his fault or hers he had failed? Oh, hell, he thought, oh, hell, oh, Hel, what is there left for us now?

And then he traced the origin of this particular uneasiness. Hel, she had said, was a special name, one that even her husband never used, and that he himself must never use in public. He had not done so. How did it happen that Felix knew the name? He remembered the conversation, which seemed long ago although it was only this morning; he even remembered the words: 'Porter's just a slob but Hel's poison.'

Desperately, like a man submerged trying to reach the surface, he strove to understand this but failed.

At the far end of the beach, jewels glittered. Were they diamonds? Through the haze of his mind came the thought that jewels are not found on beaches. If he was lying on jewels it would be proof that he was dreaming. He picked up a handful of sand, looked at it, saw that it was the characteristic powdery shingle of the coast. It did not shine, so why were diamonds flashing less than a hundred yards away?

Collect them, he thought, sell them, and he would be rich. He tried to get up, dropped on his knees again dizzily, and then managed it. Tottering like an invalid he approached the thing that shone. Half a dozen yards away he identified it. His swordstick, removed from its walking-stick sheath, was what glittered in the setting sun.

That was not surprising, for the sun always glittered on metal. But what was it doing here, and why did one end of it look dull? At the same time he noticed dark smears on his shirt.

He ran down to the sea, dipped the blade in the water. The stick itself lay a little farther back up the beach. He stared at it, stared again at the blade, began to shiver. The putt-putt of an engine came into his consciousness, and looking out to sea he saw a motor launch making for the island. A man in uniform stood in the bow, blasts sounded on a hooter.

Robin Edgley dropped to his knees and prayed that what he saw and felt might still be a dream. . .

The young Yugoslav lieutenant of police and his assistant found the woman's husband without difficulty. The body lay a few yards back from the beach in a hollow, with stab wounds through the chest. The weapon was present, the sword stick which the man Edgley had been cleaning in the water.

As for the motive, the woman herself had admitted behaving badly with Edgley when she called on them to ask for police help because she was worried that the boat had not returned. The Lieutenant found the situation both ridiculous and disgusting. One would not have supposed – this was the only surprise – that so fussy a man as this Englishman would have been capable of so vigorous a reaction.

He offered no resistance when the Lieutenant handcuffed him. They put the dead man into the other boat, and his assistant brought it back. On the return journey the Lieutenant, who was proud of the English he had learned as a second language at school, tried without success to make conversation. The Englishman said almost nothing, except when they passed Lokrum. Then he made the suggestion that a man wearing skindiving equipment could have swum from Lokrum to the island.

'It would be possible,' said the Lieutenant. 'But what man? And my dear Mr Edgley, how would he have obtained your sword? And why were you cleaning the sword when we came?'

'It is hopeless,' Edgley said, and then after a pause, 'It was all planned, of course.'

Was this a kind of religious determinism, a reference to the God in whom Edgley no doubt believed? The Lieutenant decided to make the situation clear. 'It is hopeless to attempt to deceive. But it was a crime of passion. You will find that we understand such things. You will perhaps be only five years in prison.'

The Englishman made no reply. He said only one more thing, just before they tied up in Dubrovnik harbour. The woman waited there, her gold hair visible in the dusk. A man whom the Lieutenant knew to be Edgley's cousin waited with her. Edgley then said something which the Lieutenant, in spite of his excellent English, did not understand. 'Will you please repeat that?' he asked, a little annoyed.

'A theme for Hyacinth,' Edgley said. 'It is a theme for Hyacinth alone.'

It made no better sense the second time.

THE LAST TIME

Caroline Amesbury had been married for three years before she had her first walk out with a man. She had somehow never regarded such a thing as even a possibility, and she said so when a young man at a party whose dark hair curled attractively over his collar made his feelings and intentions unmistakeable, and when she realised with astonishment that her own wishes matched his. When he laughed and said that there was always one safe place in a house or a flat she did not understand him, and not until he followed her into a dark room and slid a bolt did she realise that she was in what everybody she knew called a loo. What followed was brief but pleasurable, and part of the pleasure rested in the sense she had that for him she was a desired object, not a person. The very brevity and detachment of the thing was its charm, and when half an hour later he waved his hand, said, 'See you,' and went off with the girl he had brought to the party, she knew that she would never see him again.

So that was her first walk out – which was the out-of-date but somehow appropriate term she used, for how could you solemnly call it *adultery*? The first and the last time, she told herself, although she knew that this would not be true. The truth was that life with Bernard bored her. He had given her a pleasant house in what he called the nicest part of town and she thought of as the suburbs, and all the devotion she could have asked for, and they were not enough. Indeed, it seemed to her at times that she did not want any of the things so carefully provided. It did not help that when she expressed discontent Bernard was immediately sympathetic, and encouraged her to get the part-time job with a magazine that was an inadequate substitute for children. She was astonished when the chairman of the electronics firm in which Bernard was the general manager said that they valued above all things his decisiveness, for it often seemed to her that she was married to a rubber sponge.

She did not say these things to other people. After the chairman's visit, Bernard told her that he had been full of praise for her skill as a hostess and her charm as a woman. 'He said I ought to look after you carefully and I told him that I certainly meant to,' he said with the boyishly modest laugh that she had once adored and now found so irritating. When he put his hand on hers and said, 'I do know how lucky I am, darling,' she could have screamed, although in fact she smiled and said she was glad to have met with the chairman's approval. Later she looked at the small delicate face framed in blonde hair that the mirror reflected back at her, and wondered what the chairman would say if he knew the things she did. But nobody knew, she told nobody, except of course Jane.

Jane had been with her at the conventional, moderately grand girls' boarding school Caroline had attended, a figure increasingly seen as absurd as she dashed down the field the wrong way at lacrosse or found difficulty in lacing up the ghastly shoes they had to wear. Only in the school plays did Jane shine. At first she played awkward masculine parts like Tony Lumpkin, but she showed an unexpected flexibility of speech and style, and by the end of Caroline's schooldays had graduated to Lady Macbeth.

Well, that was Jane, who had come home with her often at school holidays. These were always rather a drag because Caroline's mother had died when she was small and her father, a Colonel in the Royal Engineers, often made it clear that he had not much use for a girl around the house. He had tried to teach her to ride and to shoot, and had even given her when she was sixteen a little ladies' revolver which after his death and her marriage to Bernard she kept in her memory drawer, but she had simply been no good at riding or shooting or any country pursuit. Her father was not very kind about Jane. He invented a little rhyme which went 'Caroline is perfectly fine, but poor old Jane's just a pain', which simply maddened Caroline. And after he had married again, a woman who was only ten years older than his daughter, he became totally absorbed with his new wife so that it was a relief to slope off into the woods that bounded the estate with Jane, and have long talks in the semi-darkness of the trees about things like the beastliness of her father and the things he got up to with his wife Heather. Jane was prudish, and easily shocked by these conversations. Sometimes Caroline became more outspoken than she would otherwise have been – because if she admitted it to herself the marriage had upset her – just to annoy her friend. And Jane wasn't very pleased when Caroline broke the news about Bernard. Her face took on what Caroline thought of as her cow look, obstinate and silly.

'But, Carol,' she said, 'he sounds quite nice, but I mean —' She stopped, and Caroline could not make her go on. In the end she said it herself.

'He's not our class, that's what you mean, isn't it?'

'Well, Carol, since you say so. I mean, he didn't even get to a grammar school.'

That sent her round the bend. 'God, how snobbish can you be? Compared with most of the men I meet Bernard's tough, hard, he knows what he wants. That's what I expect of a man. And you don't know what he's like, you've never even met him.'

At that Jane, obstinate cow Jane, just looked down at the ground and said like somebody pronouncing a death sentence, 'I hope you'll be happy. But I don't believe

Bernard's the sort of person you say he is.'

Jane was obviously upset by the marriage, because after it she did not put in an appearance for – how long? – oh, for eighteen months. And by that time Caroline had reluctantly to admit that she had been right. Bernard was not what she had believed. He was not tough but humble, aware of the honour done him by moving several steps up the social scale and by having a wife like Caroline. When they discovered that she could not have a child because of some strange tangled-up condition of her ovaries, and she wept and wept as it seemed for weeks, he was endlessly tolerant. He understood, understood only too well, when she got depressed and had blinding headaches. At the office he did not push himself forward as she thought he should, although he did advance almost imperceptibly up to the position of general manager. Altogether, he was one of nature's rubber sponges.

Jane had been so beastly about Bernard that Caroline was determined to keep her away from him. This determination was not changed by the discovery, when she turned up again after the lapse of eighteen months, that Jane had now taken to wearing mannish clothes and was obviously less prepared to be Caroline's doormat than she had been in the past. It was with something like a sneer that Jane asked how things were going, and almost with brutality that she said, 'So the working class boy didn't come up to scratch.'

Caroline felt at once the instinct to defend him. 'He's nice, I won't let you say anything against Bernard. It isn't Bernard, it's me. I mean, I'm an awful bitch, I don't think I ought to have got married.' Jane smiled slightly, reacting only when Caroline said gloomily, 'I believe I'm frigid.'

'You're not frigid,' Jane said angrily. 'Don't you believe it.' Although of course she didn't know.

Anyway, it was Jane she told about the young man at

the party, and about the others. Once she had understood that little walk outs were possible, and that if they were managed discreetly Bernard need not know about them – for she did like Bernard, faithful St Bernard, and even though he sometimes bored her she would not have wanted to hurt him – they became more frequent. The revelation that had come to her through the young man with dark attractively curling hair was that all you needed was a room with a door that locked, and you could perform the act.

It was not necessary to remove your clothes, and even a bed was not necessary. In fact she did not particularly care for lying on a bed, the exciting thing was to be pushed against a wall or to be lying or kneeling on the floor, and to have the whole thing over as quickly as possible. It was exciting, but at the same time it was slightly like taking a dose of medicine, she wanted it to happen and at the same time wanted also to get it over. She became adept at making signals that men at a drinks party or a dinner party understood, and after that the routine did not vary greatly. The rather lavish lunch a few days later, the invitation, the acceptance, the room, the act. And after the act? Well, after the act was, as they said in the old books, a let down. Sometimes she quite literally and disconcertingly could not understand what she had been doing in a room with a part-naked hairy-legged man who looked at her strangely. They would get dressed, often without speaking, she would leave the man's flat or the hotel in which he had booked a room, and that little walk out would be over. The last time, she would say to herself as she hurried home to Bernard, that's positively the last time. Apart from anything else, there was the chance that he would find out. She tried to be as careful as possible, and to confine herself to men she met through her office work, but there were two who knew them socially and had actually come to their house. Bernard looked at her very oddly sometimes, and she wondered if he suspected or even knew, but his invariably gentle manner towards her did not change.

Discussing the whole thing with Jane, Caroline put the question: was she a nymphomaniac? They talked in Caroline's bedroom, of course, when Bernard was at the office. Jane had now taken to smoking small cigars, which she chewed on like a man. She snorted like a man too, as she said that Caroline was talking rubbish.

'First you say you're frigid, now you're a nympho. I'll tell you what's the trouble with you, my girl. You just haven't met the right man.' And Jane spat, actually spat, as though she were the right man herself.

'Do you think it's really that? I just don't know anything any more.' Caroline to her dismay found herself crying. Jane made consoling noises. After she had gone Caroline realised that the room stank of cigar smoke and opened the windows, but Bernard's sense of smell was acute and almost as soon as he opened the door he asked who had been there. When she said nobody – for Bernard had never met Jane and it would have been too difficult to tell him about her – he became, for Bernard, quite annoyed. He said that somebody had smoked a cigar and actually went round looking for the butt, which fortunately she had put into the waste destructor. His suspicions did not seem to be allayed, he kept looking strangely at her for the whole evening.

It was in the following week that she met Victor, and went with him to a hotel, and lay down there with him upon a bed, and knew that this was something new and different in her life and not just another walk out. Victor was a media man in an advertising agency, and she met him at a conference. At the conference he was easy and smiling but masterful, and later on when he took her to lunch and asked about herself and her life he did so like somebody genuinely interested, and not just a man trying to make a pretty woman. She felt herself flowering under the warmth of his sympathy.

In almost every respect he was unlike her previous walk outs. He was ten years older than she, whereas they had all been younger, and he looked his age with streaks of grey in his dark hair, and vertical lines of care marking his face. He was married and had two children, whose pictures he carried in his wallet. If somebody else had told her about Victor she might have thought him fairly dismal, but in fact he had the total composure of somebody who knew exactly what he wanted, and when. On this first meeting he did not touch her, did not even kiss her goodbye, but arranged another lunch date. The next time they met in the lounge of the biggest hotel in the city and he said simply, 'I don't think we want lunch, do we? I've kept the cab,' and they went straight to a small hotel. He made love with a mixture of force and tenderness, telling her exactly what to do but with a concern also for pleasing her. Such a concern was unknown to Bernard or to the walk outs, so that the whole thing was not at all like taking medicine. When it was over she wept and kissed his hand. She did not think of hurrying home to Bernard, and it was Victor eventually who looked at his watch, said that he must put in an appearance at the office and arranged to meet her in three days' time. The second time she had the same feeling of fulfilment, and she knew that her life was changed.

She found herself reluctant to tell Jane about Victor, but that perceptive remark about not having found the right man made her do so. But Jane – who had become a rather objectionable confidant, always sneering and contemptuous – was concerned, as she might have expected, to belittle Victor. Caroline protested. She really had met the right man.

'I daresay. But are you the right woman? Just take a look in the glass.' Caroline did so. Certainly there was something hectic and strained about her appearance. Jane went on jeeringly, 'You're not so bad now, but you should see yourself sometimes.'

Caroline snapped back. 'It's better than looking and behaving like a man. You want to look at *yourself.* You're – well, almost a freak.'

'Let me tell you something. Within a month he'll have said goodbye. Given you the push. And what will our pretty Caroline do then, poor thing?'

'He's not *like* that,' Caroline almost screeched.

'Isn't he? If I met him I'd tell him a few things.'

'I'll tell you something,' Caroline said more calmly. 'You never will.'

She felt that she had won the argument, but she was still upset by it. That evening Bernard asked if she felt all right, and when she said yes, he talked about going away for a holiday. In the next breath he added, 'I know I often get on your nerves. I don't mean to, but I do. Anyway, I couldn't manage to get away just now. I thought a couple of weeks on your own, down in Devon or Cornwall perhaps —'

'Yes,' she said. 'Oh yes, what a wonderful idea.' She saw the prospect of two whole weeks with Victor. Belatedly she added, 'Of course, I'd like it if you could come.'

Bernard looked sad and petulant as he said truthfully that she didn't want him.

On the next day she was so excited that she telephoned Victor at his office, something he had told her never to do. His voice on the telephone was neutral, guarded, as he agreed to meet her the next day. They went straight to the hotel and there he was coldly angry, unmoved by tears.

'I'm sorry, but I was so excited. I had to tell you, don't you see?'

'You must have known I can't come away with you just like that.' She did not reply. 'You must realise it's impossible.'

To check the hateful words she dragged him on to the bed, unzipped and kissed him, started to take off her clothes. Later he said, 'I might be able to manage a weekend.'

'Only a weekend?'

'Even that would be difficult.'

'I love you.'

'I love you too.'

'Then you'll manage it. Somehow.'

'I want to, you know that. Look, Caroline —'

'Yes.'

'I've got a wife, you've got a husband. How about them?'

'They can pair off if they want to,' she said, giggling as though she were drunk. He looked at her without smiling.

That was Friday. On Tuesday they met again, and she told him that she was going on the next Saturday to a little village in south Devon. She traced a finger on his chest, which was covered with grey hair. 'When will you come?'

'I don't think I can.'

'But you said you would.'

'I said I'd try. It's going to be too difficult.' She tugged at the grey hair. 'Don't do that, Caroline, I think we ought to stop seeing each other.'

She stared at him, amazed, horrified. 'Why?'

'I think we should, that's all. I don't want Monica to find out, you don't want your Bernard to know.'

'But I don't care,' she said. 'I'll tell him, I want to tell him.'

He was putting on his shirt and tie, and spoke with his back to her. 'If you think I'm going to tell Monica, you're a fool.' He turned, saw her stricken face, spoke gently. 'I'm sorry, Caro. But you must see. This had better be the last time.'

At that she cried out and wept and pleaded, until he agreed to see her on Friday, the day before she went. He brushed aside her thanks. 'It won't make any difference.' But there he was wrong.

It was impossible for her to tell Bernard, so she told Jane. And then the memory of those earlier words came back to her, about meeting Victor and telling him a few things.

He was waiting for her in the little lounge of the hotel, and he did not comment on her appearance until they were in the bedroom. Then he said, 'What in God's name have you been doing to yourself?'

'That's not the right question, is it? The question is, what are you going to do with Caroline?'

'I don't understand you.' He really did look bewildered.

'Are you going away with her?'

'I – please –'

'You're not. I can tell you that here and now.'

'Why are you dressed like that?'

'Dressed like what?' she asked contemptuously. She took out and lighted a small cigar while he watched her, astonished. Then she deliberately drew from her trousers pocket the little revolver that had been for so long in her memory drawer. He just had time to stammer out some incoherent words when she began to shoot.

The noise in the small room was very loud, and there was a lot of smoke. She was still a bad shot, and one of the bullets struck the long looking-glass, so that broken glass mixed with blood on the floor. The strip of glass remaining showed a grotesque figure, evidently feminine but wearing bell-bottom trousers and a double-breasted jacket, and a cap that contained the fair hair piled on her head. A cigar stuck out of the figure's mouth, making it look like a ventriloquist's dummy.

When the police came this figure was nursing in her arms the head of the dead man. She spoke to the police quite coherently. She told them that her name was Jane, and refused to give a surname. She had shot the man because of his behaviour to her friend Caroline Amesbury. 'She wanted him to go on screwing her, and he'd had enough. Nobody does that to Caroline, not while I'm around.'

One of the policemen had been looking through her bag. He showed something to the sergeant, who nodded. He said formally, 'Caroline Jane Amesbury, I am taking you into custody on a charge of—'

The two other policemen in the room watched fascinated as the ventriloquist's dummy shrieked, leapt at the sergeant like a cat and brought him to the ground. Before they could drag her off and handcuff her she had torn his cheek badly with her nails and bitten his ear almost through. Later the hospital put five stitches in it.

'Drink your coffee.'

Celia sat feet up on the sofa reading a fashion magazine, the coffee cup on the table beside her. 'What's that?'

'I said drink your coffee. You know you like it to be piping hot.'

She contemplated the coffee, stirred it with a spoon, then put the spoon back in the saucer. 'I'm not sure it's hot enough now.'

'I poured it only a couple of minutes ago.'

'Yes, but still. I don't know that I feel like coffee tonight. But I do want a brandy.' She swung her legs off the sofa and went across to the drinks tray. 'A celebratory brandy. Can I pour one for you?'

'What are we celebrating?'

'Me, Giles, not you. I'm celebrating. But you want me to drink my coffee, don't you? All right.' She went swiftly back, lifted the coffee cup, drank the contents in two gulps and made a face. 'Not very hot. Now may I have my brandy?'

'Of course. Let me pour it for you.'

'Oh no, I'll do it myself. After all, you poured the coffee.' She smiled sweetly.

'What do you mean?'

'Just that we've both had coffee. And you poured it. But I gave it to you on the tray, remember?'

Sir Giles got up, put a hand to his throat. 'What are you trying to say?'

'Only that if I turned the tray round you'll have got my cup and I shall have got yours. But it wouldn't matter. Or would it?'

He made for the door and turned the handle, but it did not open. 'It's locked. What have you done with the key?'

'I can't imagine.' As he lumbered towards her, swaying a little, she easily evaded him. 'You think I'm a fool, Giles, don't you? I'm not, that's your mistake. So this is a celebration.'

'Celia.' His hand was at his throat again. He choked, collapsed on to the carpet and lay still.

Celia looked at him thoughtfully, finished her brandy, prodded him with her foot and said, 'Now, what to do about the body?'

The curtain came down. The first act of *Villain* was over.

'I enjoyed it enormously,' Duncan George said. 'Is it all right if I smoke?'

'Of course.' Oliver Glass was busy at the dressing table, removing the make-up that had turned him into Sir Giles. In the glass he saw Dunc packing his pipe and lighting it. Good old Dunc, he thought, reliable dull old Dunc, his reactions are always predictable. 'Pour yourself a drink.'

'Not coffee, I hope.' Oliver's laugh was perfunctory. 'I thought the play was really clever. All those twists and turns in the plot. And you enjoy being the chief actor as well as the writer, don't you, it gives you an extra kick?'

'My dear fellow, you're a psychologist as well as a crime writer yourself, you should know. But after all, who can interpret one's own writing better than oneself? The play – well, between these four walls it's a collection of tricks. The supreme trick is to make the audience accept it, to deceive them not once or twice but half-a-dozen times, to make them leave the theatre gasping at the cleverness of it all. And if that's to be done, Sir Giles has to be played on just the right note, so that we're never certain whether he's fooling everybody else or being fooled himself, never quite sure whether he's the villain or the hero. And who knows that better than the author? So if he happens to be an actor too, he must be perfect for the part.'

'Excellent special pleading. I'll tell you one thing, though. When the curtain comes down at the end of the first act, nobody really believes you're dead. Oliver Glass is the star, and if you're dead they've been cheated. So they're just waiting for you to come out of that cupboard.'

'But think of the tension that's building while they wait. Ready, Dunc.'

He clapped the other on the shoulder, and they walked out into the London night. Oliver Glass was a slim, elegant man in his fifties, successful both as actor and dramatist, so successful that he could afford to laugh at the critic who said that he had perfected the art of over-acting, and the other critic who remarked that after seeing an Oliver Glass play he was always reminded of the line that said life is mostly froth and bubble. Whether Oliver did laugh was another matter, for he disliked any adverse view of his abilities. He had a flat in the heart of the West End, a small house in Sussex, and a beautiful wife named Elizabeth who was fifteen years his junior.

Duncan George looked insignificant by his side. He was short and square, a practising psychiatrist who also wrote crime stories, and he had known Oliver for some years. He was typified for Oliver by the abbreviation of his first name, *Dunc.* He was exactly the kind of person Oliver could imagine dunking a doughnut into a cup of coffee, or doing something equally vulgar. With all that, however, Dunc was a good fellow, and Oliver tolerated him as a companion.

They made their way through the West End to a street off Leicester Square where the Criminologists' Club met once a quarter, to eat a late supper followed by a talk on a subject of criminal interest. The members were all writers about real or fictitious crime, and on this evening Oliver Glass was to speak to them on 'The Romance of Crime', with Duncan George as his chairman. When he rose and looked around, with that gracious look in which there was just a touch of contempt, the buzz of conversation ceased.

'Gentlemen,' he began, 'Criminologists, fellow crime writers, perhaps fellow criminals. I have come tonight to plead for romance in the world of crime, for the locked room murder, the impossible theft, the crime committed by the invisible man. I have come to plead that you should bring wit and style and complexity to your writings about crime, that you should remember Stevenson's view that life is a bazaar of dangerous and smiling chances, and the remark of Thomas Griffith Wainewright when he confessed to poisoning his pretty sister-in-law: 'It was a terrible thing to do, but she had thick ankles'. I beseech you not to forget those thick ankles as a motive, and to abandon the dreary books some of you write concerned with examining the psychology of two equally dull people to decide which destroyed the other, or looking at bits of intestines under a microscope to determine whether a tedious husband killed his boring wife. Your sights should be set instead on the Perfect Crime. . .'

Oliver Glass spoke, as always, without notes, fluently and with style, admiring the fluency and stylishness as the words issued from his mouth. Afterwards he was challenged by some members, Duncan George among them, about that conjectural Perfect Crime. Wasn't it out of date? Not at all, Oliver said, Sir Giles in *Villain* attempted it.

'Yes, but as you remarked yourself, *Villain*'s a mass of clever tricks,' Dunc said. 'Sir Giles wants to kill Celia as a kind of trick, just to prove that he can get away with it. Or at least, we think he does. Then you play all sorts of variations on the idea, is the poison really a sleeping draught, does she know about it, that kind of thing. Splendid to watch, but nobody would actually try it. In every perfect murder, so called, there is actually a flaw.' There was a chorus of agreement, by which Oliver found himself a little irritated.

'How do you know that? The Perfect Crime is one in which the criminal never puts himself within reach of the law. Perhaps, even, no crime is known to have taken place, although that is a little short of perfection. But how do we know, gentlemen, what variations on the Perfect Crime any of us may be planning, may even have carried out? "The desires of the heart are as crooked as corkscrews", as the poet says, and I'm sure Dunc can bear that out from his psychiatric experience.'

'Any of us is capable of violence under certain circumstances, if that's what you mean. But to set out to commit a Perfect Crime without a motive is the mark of a psychopath.'

'I didn't say without motive. A good motive for one man may be trivial to another.'

'Tell us when you're going to commit the Perfect Crime, and we'll see if we can solve it,' somebody said. There was a murmur of laughter.

Upon this note he left, and strolled home to Everley Court, passing the drunks on the pavements, the blacks and yellows and all conditions of foreigners, who jostled each other or stood gaping outside the sex cinemas. He made a slight detour to pass the theatre, and saw with a customary glow of pleasure the poster: 'Oliver Glass in *Villain*. The Mystery Play by Oliver Glass.' Was he really planning the Perfect Crime? There can be no doubt, he said to himself, that the idea is in your mind. And the elements are there, Elizabeth and deliciously unpredictable Evelyn, and above all the indispensable Eustace. But is it more than a whim? Do I really dislike Elizabeth enough? The answer to that, of course, was that it was not a question of hatred but of playing a game, the game of Oliver Glass versus Society, even Oliver Glass versus the World.

And so home. And to Elizabeth.

A nod to Tyler, the night porter at the block of flats. Up in the lift to the third floor. Key in the door.

From the entrance hall the apartment stretched left and right. To the left Elizabeth's bedroom and bathroom. Almost directly in front of him the living room, further to the right dining room and kitchen, at the extreme right Oliver's bedroom and bathroom. He went into the living room, switched on the light. On the mantelpiece there was a note in Elizabeth's scrawl: *O. Please come to see me if back before 2 a.m. E.*

For two years now they had communicated largely by means of such notes. It had begun – how had it begun? – because she was so infuriatingly talkative when he wanted to concentrate. 'I am an artist,' he had said. 'The artist needs isolation, if the fruits of genius are to ripen on the bough of inspiration.' The time had been when Elizabeth listened open-eyed to such words, but those days had gone. For a long while now she had made comments suggesting that his qualities as actor and writer fell short of genius, or had pointed out that last night he had happily stayed late at a party. She did not understand the artistic temperament. Her nagging criticism had become, quite simply, a bore.

There was, he admitted as he turned the note in his fingers, something else. There were the girls needed by the artist as part of his inspiration, the human clay turned by him into something better. Elizabeth had never understood about them, and in particularly had failed to understand when she had returned to find one of them with him on the living room carpet. She had spoken of divorce, but he knew the words to be idle. Elizabeth had extravagant tastes, and divorce would hardly allow her to indulge them. So the notes developed. They lived separate lives, with occasional evenings when she acted as hostess, or came in and chatted amiably enough to friends. For the most part the arrangement suited him rather well, although just at present his absorption with Evelyn was such. . .

He went in to see Elizabeth.

She was sitting on a small sofa, reading. Although he valued youth above all things he conceded, as he looked appraisingly at her, that she was still attractive. Her figure was slim (no children, he could not have endured the messy noisy things), legs elegant, feet dainty. She had kept her figure, as – he confirmed, looking at himself in the glass – he had kept his. How curious that he no longer found her desirable.

'Oliver.' He turned. 'Stop looking at yourself.'

'Was I doing that?'

'You know you were. Stop acting.'

'But I am an actor.'

'Acting off stage, I mean. You don't know anybody exists outside yourself.'

'There is a respectable philosophical theory maintaining that very proposition. I have invented you, you have invented me. A charming idea.'

'A very silly idea. Oliver, why don't you divorce me?'

'Have you given me cause?'

'You know how easily it can be arranged.'

He answered with a weary, a world-weary sigh. She exclaimed angrily and he gave her a look of pure dislike, so that she exclaimed again.

'You *do* dislike me, don't you? A touch of genuine feeling. So why not?' She went over to her dressing table, sat down, took out a pot of cream.

He placed a hand on his heart. 'I was –'

'I know. You were born a Catholic. But when did you last go to church?'

'Very well. Say simply that I don't care to divorce you. It would be too vulgar.'

'You've got a new girl. I can always tell.'

'Is there anything more tedious than feminine intuition?'

'Let me tell you something. This time I shall have you followed. And *I* shall divorce *you*. What do you think of that?'

'Very little.' And indeed, who would pay her charge account at Harrods, provide the jewellery she loved, above all where would she get the money she gambled away at casinos and race meetings? She had made similar threats before, and he knew them to be empty ones.

'You want me as a kind of butterfly you've stuck with a pin, nothing more.'

She was at work with the cream. She used one cream on her face, another on her neck, a third on her legs. Then she covered her face with a black mask, which was supposed to increase the effectiveness of the cream. She often kept this face cream on all night.

There had been a time when he found it exciting to make love to a woman whose face was not visible, but in her case that time had gone long ago. What was she saying now?

'Nothing gets through to you, does it? You have a sort of armour of conceit. But you have the right name, do you know that? *Glass* – if one could see through you there would be nothing, absolutely nothing there. Oliver Glass, *you don't exist.*'

Very well, he thought, very well, I am an invisible man. I accept the challenge. Elizabeth, you have signed your death warrant.

*

The idea, then, was settled. Plans had to be made. But they were still amorphous, moving around in what he knew to be his marvellously ingenious mind, when he went to visit Evelyn after lunch on the following day. Evelyn was in her early twenties, young enough – oh yes, he acknowledged it – to be his daughter, young enough also to be pleased by the company of a famous actor. But beyond that, Evelyn fascinated him by her unpredictability. She was a photographer's model much in demand, and he did not doubt that she had other lovers. There were times when she said that she was too busy to see him, or simply that she wanted to be alone, and he accepted these refusals as part of the excitement of the chase. There was a perversity about Evelyn, an abandonment to the whim of the moment, that reached out to something in his own nature. He felt sometimes that there was no suggestion so outrageous that she would refuse to consider it. She had once opened the door of her flat naked, and asked him to strip and accompany her down to the street.

Her flat was off Baker Street, and when he rang the bell there was no reply. At the third ring he felt annoyance. He had telephoned in advance, as always, and she had said she would be there. He pushed the door in a tentative way, and it swung open. In the hall he called her name. There was no reply.

The flat was not large. He went into the living room, which was untidy as usual, glanced into the small kitchen, then went into the bedroom with its unmade bed. What had happened to her, where was she? He entered the bathroom, and recoiled from what he saw.

Evelyn lay face down, half in and half out of the bath. One arm hung over the side of the bath, the other trailed in the water. Her head rested on the side of the bath as though her neck was broken.

He went across to her, touched the arm outside the bath. It was warm. He bent down to feel the pusle. As he did so the arm moved, the body turned, and Evelyn was laughing at him.

'You frightened me. You bitch.' But he was excited, not angry.

'The author of *Villain* should be used to tricks.' She got out, handed him a towel. 'Dry me.'

Their lovemaking afterwards had the frantic, paroxysmic quality that he had found in few women. It was as though he were bringing her back from the dead. A thought struck him. 'Have you done that with anybody else?'

'Does it matter?'

'Perhaps not. I should still like to know.'

'Nobody else.'

'It was as though you were another person.'

'Good. I'd like to be a different person every time.'

He was following his own train of thought. 'My wife puts on a black mask after creaming her face at night. That should be exciting, but it isn't.'

Evelyn was insatiably curious about the details of sex, and he had told her a good deal about Elizabeth.

'I'm good for you,' she said now. 'You get a kick each time, don't you?'

'Yes. And you?'

She considered this. She had a similar figure to Elizabeth's but her features were very different, the nose snub instead of aquiline, the eyes blue and wide apart. 'In a way. Being who you are gives me a kick.'

'Is that all?'

'What do you mean?'

'Don't you like me?'

'It's wet to ask things like that. I never thought you were

wet.' She looked at him directly with her large, slightly vacant blue eyes. 'If you want to know, I get a kick out of you because you're acting all the time. It's the acting you like, not the act. And then I get a kick out of you being an old man.'

He was so angry that he slapped her face. She said calmly, 'Yes, I like that too.'

By the time that night's performance was over his plan was made.

In the next two weeks Tyler, the night porter at Everley Court, was approached three times by a tall, bulky man wearing horn-rimmed spectacles. The man asked for Mrs Glass, and seemed upset to learn on every occasion that she was out. Once he handed a note to Tyler and then took it back, saying that it wouldn't do to leave a letter lying around. Twice he left messages, to say that Charles had called and wanted to talk to Mrs Glass. On his third visit the man smelled of drink, and his manner was belligerent. 'You tell her I must talk to her,' he said in an accent that Tyler could not place, except that the man definitely came from somewhere up north.

'Yes, sir. And the name is —'

'Charles. She'll know.'

Tyler coughed. 'Begging your pardon, sir, but wouldn't it be better to telephone?'

The man glared at him. 'Do you think I haven't tried? You tell her to get in touch. If she doesn't I won't answer for the consequences.'

'Charles?' Elizabeth said when Tyler rather hesitantly told her this. 'I know two or three people named Charles, but this doesn't seem to fit any of them. What sort of age?'

'Perhaps about forty, Mrs Glass. Smartly dressed. A gentleman. Comes from the north, maybe Scotland, if that's any help.'

'No doubt it should be, but it isn't.'

'He seemed —' Tyler hesitated. 'Very concerned.'

On the following day Oliver left a note for her. *E. Man rang while you were out, wouldn't leave message. O.* She questioned him about the call.

'He wouldn't say what he wanted. Just rang off when I said you weren't here.'

'It must be the same man.' She explained about him. 'Tyler said he had a northern accent, probably Scottish.'

'What Scots do you know named Charles?'

'Charlie Rothsey, but I haven't seen him for years. I wish he'd ring when I'm here.'

A couple of evenings later the wish was granted, although she did not speak to the man. Oliver had asked her to give a little supper party after the show for three members of the cast, and because two of them were women Duncan was invited to even up the numbers. Elizabeth was serving the cold salmon when the telephone rang in the living room. Oliver went to answer it. He came back almost at once, looking thoughtful. When Elizabeth said it had been a quick call, he looked sharply at her. 'It was your friend Charles. He rang off. Just announced himself, then rang off when he heard my voice.'

'Who's Charles?' one of the women asked. 'He sounds interesting.'

'You'd better ask Elizabeth.'

She told the story of the man who had called, and it caused general amusement. Only Oliver remained serious. When the guests were going he asked Duncan to stay behind.

'I just wanted your opinion, Dunc. This man has called three times and now he's telephoning. What sort of man would do this kind of thing, and what can we do about it?'

'What sort of man? Hard to say.' Duncan took out his pipe, filled and lit it with maddening deliberation. 'Could be a practical joker, harmless enough. Or it could be somebody – well, not so harmless. But I don't see that you can do much about it. Obscene and threatening phone calls are ten a penny, as the police will tell you. Of course if he does show up again Elizabeth could see him, but I'd recommend having somebody else here.'

This was, Oliver considered, adequate preparation of the ground. It had been established that Elizabeth was being pursued by a character named Charles. There was no doubt about Charles's existence. He obviously existed independently of Oliver Glass, since Tyler had seen him and Oliver himself had spoken to him on the telephone. If Elizabeth was killed, the mysterious Charles would be the first suspect.

Charles had been created as somebody separate from Oliver by that simplicity which is the essence of all fine art. Oliver, like Sir Giles in *Villain*, was a master of disguise. He had in particular the ability possessed by the great Vidocq, of varying his height by twelve inches or more. Charles had been devised from a variety of props like cheek pads, body cushions and false eyebrows, plus the indispensable platform heels. He would make one more appearance, and then vanish from the scene. He would never have to meet anybody who knew Oliver well, something which was slightly to be regretted. And Charles on the telephone had been an actor whom Oliver had asked to ring during the evening. Oliver had merely said he couldn't talk now but would call him tomorrow, and then put down the receiver.

In the next few days he noticed with amusement tinged with annoyance that Elizabeth had fulfilled her threat of putting a private enquiry agent on his track. He spotted the man hailing a taxi just after he had got one himself, and then getting out a few yards behind him when he stopped outside Evelyn's flat. Later he pointed out the man to Evelyn, standing in a doorway opposite. She giggled, and suggested that they should ask him up.

'I believe you would,' he said admiringly. 'Is there anything you wouldn't do?'

'If I felt like it, nothing.' She was high on some drug or other. 'What about you?'

'A lot of things.'

'*Careful* old Oliver.' What would she say if she knew what he was planning? He was tempted to say something but resisted, although so far as he could tell nothing would shock her. She suddenly threw up the window, leaned out and gave a piercing whistle. When the man looked up she beckoned. He turned his head and then began to walk away Oliver was angry, but what was the use of saying anything? It was her recklessness that fascinated him.

His annoyance was reflected in a note left for Elizabeth. *E. This kind of spying is degrading. O.* He found a reply that night when he came back from the theatre. *O. Your conduct is degrading. Your present fancy is public property. E.*

That Oliver Glass had charm was acknowledged even by those not susceptible to it. In the days after the call from Charles he exerted this charm upon Elizabeth. She went out a good deal in the afternoons, where or with whom he really didn't care, and this gave him the chance to leave little notes. One of them ran: *E. You simply MUST be waiting here for me after the theatre. I have a small surprise for you. O.,* and another: *E. Would supper at Wheeler's amuse you this evening? Remembrance of things past. . .O.* On the first occasion he gave her a pretty ruby ring set with pearls, and the reference in the second note was to the fact that they had often eaten at Wheeler's in the early months after marriage. On these evenings he set out to dazzle and amuse her as he had done in the past, and she responded. Perhaps the response was unwilling, but that no doubt was because of Evelyn. He noticed, however, that the man following him was no longer to be seen, and at their Wheeler's supper mentioned this to her.

'I know who she is. I know you've always been like that. Perhaps I have to accept it.' Her eyes flashed. 'Although if I want to get divorce evidence it won't be difficult.'

'An artist needs more than one woman,' Oliver said. 'But you must not think that I can do without you. I need you. You are a fixed point in a shifting world.'

'What nonsense I do talk,' he said to himself indulgently. The truth was that contact with her nowadays was distasteful to him. By the side of Evelyn she was insipid. A great actor, however, can play any part, and this one would not be maintained for long.

Only one faintly disconcerting thing happened in this, as he thought of it, second honeymoon period. He came back to the flat unexpectedly early one afternoon, and heard Elizabeth's voice on the telephone. She replaced the receiver as he entered the room. Her face was flushed. When he asked who she had been speaking to, she said, 'Charles.'

'Charles?' For a moment he could not think who she was talking about. Then he stared at her. Nobody knew better than he that she could not have been speaking to Charles, but of course he could not say that.

'What did he say?'

'Beastly things. I put down the receiver.'

Why was she lying? How absurd, how deliciously absurd, if she had a lover. Or was it possible that somebody at the supper party was playing a practical joke? He brushed aside such conjectures because they did not matter now. Nothing could interfere with the enactment of the supreme drama of his life.

Celia's intention in *Villain* was to explain Sir Giles's

absence by saying that he had gone away on a trip, something he did from time to time. Hence the remark about disposition of the body at the end of Act One. Just after the beginning of the second act the body was revealed by Celia to her lover shoved into a cupboard, a shape hidden in a sack. A few minutes later the cupboard was opened again, and the shape was seen by the audience, although not by Celia, to move slightly. Then, after twenty-five minutes of the second act, there was a brief blackout on stage. When the lights went up Sir Giles emerged from the cupboard, not dead but drugged.

To be enclosed within a sack for that length of time is no pleasure, and in any ordinary theatrical company the body in the sack would have been that of the understudy, with the leading man changing over only a couple of minutes before he was due to emerge from the cupboard. But Oliver believed in what he called the theatre of the actual. In another play he had insisted that the voice of an actress shut up for some time in a trunk must be real and not a recording, so that the actress herself had to be in the trunk. In *Villain* he maintained that the experience of being actually in the sack was emotionally valuable, so that he always stayed in it for the whole length of time it was in the cupboard.

The body in the sack was to provide Oliver with an unbreakable alibi. The interval after Act One lasted fifteen minutes, so that he had nearly forty minutes free. Everley Court was seven minutes' walk from the theatre, and he did not expect to need much more than twenty minutes all told. The body in the sack would be seen to twitch by hundreds of people, and who could be in it but Oliver?

In fact Useful Eustace would be the sack's occupant.

Eustace was a dummy used by stage magicians who wanted to achieve very much the effect at which Oliver aimed, of persuading an audience that a human being was inside a container. He was made of plastic, and inflated to the size of a small man. You then switched on a mechanism which made Eustace kick out arms and legs in a galvanic manner. A battery-operated timer in his back could be set to work at intervals ranging from thirty seconds to five minutes. When deflated, Eustace folded up neatly, into a size no larger than a plastic mackintosh.

Eustace was the perfect accomplice, Useful Eustace indeed. Oliver had tried him out half a dozen times inside a sack of similar size, and he looked most convincing.

On the afternoon of The Day he rested. Elizabeth was out, but said that she would be back before seven. His carefully worded note was left on her mantelpiece. *E. I want you at the flat ALL this evening. A truly sensational surprise for you. All the evening, mind, not just after the show. O.* Her curiosity would not, he felt sure, be able to resist such a note.

During Act One he admired, with the detachment of the artist, his own performance. He was cynical, ironic, dramatic – in a word, superb. When it was over he went unobtrusively to his dressing room. He had no fear of visitors, for he was known to detest any interruption during the interval.

And now came what in advance he felt to be the only ticklish part of the operation. The cupboard with the sack in it opened on to the back of the stage. The danger of carrying out an inflated Eustace from dressing room to stage was too great – he must be inflated on site, as it were, and it was possible although unlikely that a wandering stage hand might see him at work. The Perfect Crime does not depend upon chance or upon the taking of risks, and if the worst happened, if he was seen obviously inflating a dummy, the project must be abandoned for the present time. But fortune favours the creative artist, or did so on this occasion. Inflation of Eustace by pump took only a few moments as he knelt by the cupboard, and nobody came near. The timer had been set for movement every thirty seconds. He put Eustace into the sack, waited to see him twitch, closed the cupboard's false back, and strolled away.

He left the theatre by an unobtrusive exit used by those who wanted to avoid the autograph hunters outside the stage door, and walked along head down until he reached the nearest Underground station, one of the few in London equipped with lockers and lavatories. Unhurriedly he took Charles's clothes and shoes from the locker, went into a lavatory, changed, put his acting clothes back in the locker. Spectacles and revolver were in his jacket pocket. He had bought the revolver years ago, when he had been playing a part in which he was supposed to be an expert shot. By practice in a shooting range he had in fact become a quite reasonable one.

As he left the station he looked at his watch. Six minutes. Very good.

Charles put on a pair of grey gloves from another jacket pocket. Three minutes brought him to Everley Court. He walked straight across to the lift, something he could not do without being observed by Tyler. The man came over, and in Charles's husky voice, with its distinctive accent, he said: 'Going up to Mrs Glass. Expecting me.'

'I'll ring, sir. It's Mr Charles, isn't it?'

'No need. I said, she's expecting me.'

Perfectly, admirably calm. But in the lift he felt, quite suddenly, that he would be unable to do it. To allow Elizabeth to divorce him and then to marry or live with Evelyn until they tired of each other, wouldn't that after all be the sensible, obvious thing? But to be *sensible*, to be *obvious*, were such things worthy of Oliver Glass? Wasn't the whole point that by this death, which in a practical sense was needless, he would show the character of a great artist and a great actor, a truly superior man?

The lift stopped. He got out. The door confronted him. Put key in lock, turn. Enter.

The flat was in darkness, no light in the hall. No sound. 'Elizabeth,' he called, in a voice that did not seem his own. He had difficulty in not turning and leaving the flat.

He opened the door of the living room. This was also in darkness. Was Elizabeth not there after all, had she ignored his note or failed to return? He felt a wave of relief at the thought, but still there was the bedroom. He must look in the bedroom.

The door was open, a glimmer of light showed within. He did not remember taking the revolver from his pocket, but it was in his gloved hand.

He took two steps into the room. Her dimmed bedside light was switched on. She lay on the bed naked, the black mask over her face. He called out something and she sat up, stretched out arms to him. His reaction was one of disgust and horror. He was not conscious of squeezing the trigger, but the revolver in his hand spoke three times.

She did not call out but gave a kind of gasp. A patch of darkness showed between her breasts. She sank back on the bed.

With the action taken, certainty returned to him. Everything he did now was efficient, exact. He got into the lift, took it down to the basement and walked out through the garage down there, meeting nobody. Tyler would be able to say when Mr Charles had arrived, but not when he left.

Back to the Underground lavatory, clothes changed, Charles's clothing and revolver returned to locker for later disposal, locker key put in handkerchief pocket of jacket. Return to the theatre, head down to avoid recognition. A quick glance at his watch as he opened the back door and moved silently up the stairs. Nearly thirty minutes had passed.

He knelt at the back of the cupboard and listened to a few lines of dialogue. The moment at which the body was due to give its twitch had gone, and Eustace proved his lasting twitching capacity by giving another shudder, of course not seen by the audience because the cupboard door was closed. Eustace had served his purpose. Oliver withdrew him from the sack and switched him off. With slight pressure to get out the air he was quickly reduced and folded into a bundle. Oliver slipped the bundle inside his trousers, and secured it with a safety pin. The slight bulge might have been apparent on close examination, but who would carry out such an examination upon stage?

Beautiful, he thought, as he wriggled into the sack for the few minutes before he had to appear on stage. Oliver Glass, I congratulate you in the name of Thomas de Quincy and Thomas Griffiths Wainewright. You have committed the Perfect Crime.

The euphoria lasted through the curtain calls and his customary few casual words with the audience, in which he congratulated them on being able to appreciate an intelligent mystery. It lasted – oh, how he was savouring the only real achievement of his life – while he leisurely removed Sir Giles's makeup, said goodnight, and left the theatre still with Eustace pinned to him. He made one further visit to the Underground, as a result of which Eustace joined Charles's clothes in the locker. The key went back in the handkerchief pocket.

As he was walking back to Everley Court, however, he realised with a shock that something had been forgotten. The note! The note which said positively that he would be at the flat during the interval, a note which if the police saw it would certainly lead to uncomfortable questions, perhaps even to a search and discovery of the locker key. The note was somewhere in the flat, perhaps in

Elizabeth's bag. It must be destroyed before he rang the police.

He nodded to Tyler, took the lift up. Key in door again. The door open. Then he stopped.

Light gleamed under the living room door.

Impossible, he thought, impossible. I know that I did not switch on the light when I opened that door. But then who could be inside the room? He took two steps forward, turned the handle, and when the door was open sprang back with a cry.

'Why, Oliver. What's the matter?' Elizabeth said. She sat on the sofa. Duncan stood beside her.

He pulled at his collar, feeling as though he was about to choke, then tried to ask a question but could not utter words.

'Come and see,' Duncan said. He approached and took Oliver by the arm. Oliver shook his head, resisted, but in the end let himself be led to the bedroom. The body still lay there, the patch of red between the breasts.

'You even told her about Elizabeth's bedtime habits,' Dunc said. 'She must have thought you'd have some fun.' He lifted the black mask. Evelyn looked up at him.

Back in the living room he poured himself brandy and said to Elizabeth, 'You knew?'

'Of course. *Would supper at Wheeler's amuse you this evening?* Do you think I didn't know you were acting as you always are, making some crazy plan. Though I could never have believed – it was Dunc who guessed how crazy it was.'

He looked from one of them to the other. 'You're lovers?' Duncan nodded. 'My dreary wife and my dull old friend Dunc – a perfect pair.'

Duncan took out his pipe, looked at it, put it back in his pocket. 'Liz had kept me in touch with what was going on, naturally. It seemed that you must be going to do something or other tonight. So Liz spent the evening with me.'

'Why was Evelyn here?' His mind moved frantically from one point to another to see where he had gone wrong.

'We knew about her from having you watched, and all that nonsense about Charles made me think that Elizabeth must be in some sort of danger. So it seemed a good idea to send your note to Evelyn, so that she could be here to greet you. We put the flat key in the envelope.'

'The initials were the same.'

'Just so,' Dunc said placidly.

'You planned for me to kill her.'

'I wouldn't say that. Of course if you happened to mistake her for Liz – but we couldn't guess that she'd put on Liz's mask. We just wanted to warn you that playing games is dangerous.'

'You can't prove anything.'

'Oh, I think so,' Dunc said sagely. 'I don't know how you managed to get away from the theatre, some sort of dummy in the sack I suppose? No doubt the police will soon find out. But the important thing is that note. It's in Evelyn's handbag. Shows you arranged to meet her here. Jealous of some younger lover, I suppose.'

'But I *wasn't* jealous, I didn't arrange —' He stopped.

'Can't very well say it was for Liz, can you? Not when Evelyn turned up.' The door bell rang. 'Oh, I forgot to say we called the police when we found the body. Our duty, you know.' He looked at Oliver and said reflectively, 'You remember I said there was always a flaw in the Perfect Crime? Perhaps I was wrong. I suppose you might say the Perfect Crime is one you benefit from but don't commit yourself, so that nobody can say you're responsible. Do you see what I mean?' Oliver saw what he meant. 'And now it's time to let in the police.'

LOVE AFFAIR

From the beginning of their marriage it had always been Don who made the decisions and, as Moira told their friends, this was not because he was aggressive or domineering, it was just that both of them thought it right and natural for things to be that way. When, after a year of marriage, he suggested that it was time they moved from the little flat in Kilburn to a district where you could see a bit more of God's green earth and sky, she agreed at once.

He ticked off on his fingers just what they wanted: a three- or four-bedroom house, central heating, a garden big enough to sit in, and of course the whole thing set in a nice place with neighbours who were their own sort.

She agreed with it all. But wouldn't a garden mean a lot of work?

'I'll look after it. Always fancied myself with the old spade and trowel.' Tamping down the tobacco in his pipe, not looking at her, Don said, 'And you need a bit of garden for the kids.'

'But you said we ought to wait.'

'Got a bit of news. MacGillivray's retiring. I get a step up next month.'

'Oh, Don! Why didn't you tell me?'

'Best not to say anything till you're sure. What you don't know won't hurt you, that's my motto.' He had got his pipe going. 'I've been in touch with a few estate agents already.'

It proved more difficult than they had expected to find exactly what they wanted, but when they saw the house at Gainham Woods they knew it was just the thing. It was a new development – you didn't call it an estate any more –

but the thing that made this particular house a snip, as Don said, was its position on a corner, so that you faced two ways, had more windows than your neighbours, and a bigger garden as well.

There was an attached garage, which Don said would come in handy as a workshop or playroom since they had no car. Gainham Woods was half an hour from central London by train, but Don worked out that the cost of extra fare would be balanced by the fact that living would be less expensive. And, of course, the house would run itself, so that Moira could keep her secretarial job.

'For the time being,' Don said with a smile. 'Later on you'll have your hands full.'

She did stay in the job until she was nearly three months' pregnant. After that she had rather a bad time, with a good deal of morning sickness, so she gave up the job. At six months she had a miscarriage. She was disturbed, partly because she felt it showed her incompetence, but Don was very sympathetic and told her to look on the bright side. Perhaps it would have been a bit soon anyway, and they were still young, they would try again.

When she had her second miscarriage he said that perhaps they weren't meant to have children. She had not gone back to her job because it hardly seemed worthwhile, and after the second miscarriage she found that she didn't really want to work again.

It was at this point that Tess arrived. She was a nice little black sedan, three years old but for that reason a real bargain. Don lifted the hood and expatiated on the cleanliness of what lay inside.

'It's lovely.' Then Moira added doubtfully, 'But can we afford it?'

'Have I ever bought anything we couldn't afford?' Don asked, and it was perfectly true that he never had. It turned out that he had received another minor promotion and was now an Assistant Personnel Officer in the large corporation for which he worked. He proudly showed her the name 'Tess' which he had stuck onto the side of the car with plastic letters. It was one of several names they had talked about for the baby.

There could be no doubt that Tess was a boon and a blessing. They took her occasionally on trips to the seaside, and were able to visit Don's family at weekends. His father was a retired bank manager and lived with his wife in a semi-detached house at Elmers End, a pleasant enough house but, as Don said every time they left, you couldn't compare Elmers End with Gainham Woods.

Sometimes Don's brother and sister also came to Elmers End. They were both married, and it was a real family party. Moira had no family, or none that was ever mentioned. Her father, a grocer, had gone off with another woman when Moira was in her teens, and after his departure her mother had taken gas. Of course, Moira could not be held responsible for any of this, but she always felt that the Bradburys thought their son had married beneath him.

Don had already passed his driving test – one of the things Moira had admired about him from their first meeting at the Conservative Club dance was his competence in practical matters; but she couldn't drive. As he said, there was no point in wasting money going to a school when he could easily teach her how. It would be a pleasure, he said, and on the first day that she sat in the driver's seat, with Don beside her explaining the gears and saying that there was nothing to it, not really, but it *was* just a bit tricky going from third down to second gear, she thought it might be a pleasure too, but this did not prove to be the case.

Don was immensely patient – that was another of the things she had always admired in him – but it took her a long time to understand just when and how to shift gears. First gear was close to reverse, and she frequently engaged one when she meant to use the other. And somehow Don's habit of treating every drive as an adventure didn't help.

'You see that Austin up ahead there,' he would say. 'Just crawling along. We're going to pass that fellow. Get ready now. Up into top, arm out to show you're passing, and away we go! No, steady now, something coming the other way, tuck yourself in behind him – right. Now, road's clear, give her all you've got.' And as they passed the car he would beam. 'Managed that all right though you went out too far, nearly had us in the ditch.'

'I'm sorry.'

'Nothing to worry about. Turn down this side road – no, left, not right. And you didn't give an arm signal.'

'I shall never be able to do it! There's so *much* to remember.'

'Don't worry. If at first you don't succeed, try, try again – as Confucius says. Now, this road takes us back into town and when we're back we'll try some low-gear practice.'

After six weeks of lessons he said she was ready to take her test. A day or two before it was due, however, she misinterpreted something he told her, turned left instead of right, and then stalled the engine. When she started up again, she confused reverse with first and drove straight into a tree. While Don got out to look at the damage she sat over the steering wheel and wept.

'Poor old girl.' He was addressing the car. 'She's had a nasty knock. Buckled her bumper.' He came back and patted Moira's shoulder. 'Never mind. Worse things happen at sea. Shall I drive back?'

She got out. 'I never want to drive that bloody car again!'

'Now, now, it's not her fault.' He patted the hood, got in,

and turned on the ignition. The motor hummed. 'She's a good old girl, Tess is.'

It proved possible to beat out the buckled bumper, and when it was resprayed you couldn't tell that anything had happened. At least, that was what Don said, but she caught him occasionally giving comparative glances at the bumpers, and she knew that for him the repaired one didn't look *quite* the same as the rest of the car. When he mentioned her taking the test she shook her head. 'No, I won't take it. I don't want to drive that car, ever – I hate it!'

'You're being hysterical.' It was his severest term of condemnation. 'But perhaps it would be a good thing to delay taking the test for the time being.'

'I shall never drive it again.'

Four years had passed since then and Moira had kept her word. They still had Tess – who was getting, as Don said, a bit long in the tooth but was a gallant old girl. He spent a good deal of time with the car, cleaning it inside and out every week, making adjustments in the carburettor, checking the spark plugs. She was in beautiful condition, except that the gears had become a little dicky. They had a tendency to slip, and there were even a couple of occasions when Don himself had shifted into reverse instead of into first, although he always caught himself in time. He was shocked when she suggested that they should buy another car.

'Get rid of Tess, you wouldn't want to do that! There's a lot of life in her yet, before she's ready to be put on the junk heap.'

But although Moira had not driven Tess again, she had passed her driving test. She saved a pound a week of the money Don gave her every month for household expenses, took lessons at a local driving school, and passed the test the first time. She never told him about this, partly because he would have been upset, partly because – well, she couldn't have said exactly why, but it was a thing she had done entirely on her own and she wanted to nurse her feeling of achievement.

It was after this small achievement that she found herself looking at her husband with a more critical eye. She became conscious of the fact that his sandy hair was rapidly thinning, and what had once appeared to her as profound or witty remarks now seemed obvious clichés. Also his devotion to doing everything in a certain way ('there's one right way and a thousand wrong ones') which she used to admire so much now seemed to her a childish insistence on routine. Why, for example, did he always come home on the six fifteen train, she asked, why not sometimes take an earlier one? He assumed what she regarded as his wounded expression.

'There's work to be done, my dear. A.H. himself never leaves before five thirty.'

'Just sometimes – say, once a month. You can't tell me A.H. would mind that?' A.H. was Head of Personnel.

'I daresay not. But it wouldn't be quite the thing.'

'Or catch a later one then – have a drink with the boys.'

'I don't see the point. The next one's the six forty-seven, and the six fifteen's a better train. Mind you, if there's a reason why I should get off earlier one day I can manage it – no problem there. Did you have something in mind?'

'No, no, nothing at all. It doesn't matter.'

You've become middle-aged at thirty, she thought, and I'm still young at twenty seven. The mirror, which showed a neat little figure and a pretty, slightly discontented, and somehow unused face, did not contradict her. She had hair which Don had called Titian when they first met, and a white milky skin.

In Gainham Woods, where she saw nobody except the neighbours, most of whom had children, these things were being wasted, but when she suggested that they might move nearer to London he was astounded. It was healthy out here, the neighbourhood was pleasant, you could see green things growing. They would never get a place with such a good garden. He had become devoted to gardening and had recently bought a whole set of gleaming new chromium-headed tools, including a special hoe and a rake whose sharp tines shone like silver. These tools hung neatly on the rear wall of the garage, just behind the car. What was the point of moving? he asked. Besides, they couldn't afford it.

'What about when you get moved up to become A.H.'s deputy?' Two years earlier he had told her that this was likely.

'Yes, well.' He hesitated.

'You'll get more money then.' He said nothing. 'You mean you won't get the job?'

'Salisbury's had a step up.'

Salisbury was another Assistant Personnel Officer, and Don's deadly rival.

'He's been made Deputy?' she persisted.

'In a way. There's been a reorganization.'

'But he's moved up and you stay where you are.'

'At the moment. I think A.H. may have something special in mind for me. In any position you're really dealing with people, man to man. That's my strength, as A.H. says. Salisbury's really just an administrator.'

'But he gets more money?'

'I tell you, there may be something special ahead for me. In a year or two.'

He looked away as he spoke and she knew that there was nothing special ahead for him, that he was a nonentity who had climbed the short way he would ever go up the ladder of success. When he added that he would get his yearly increase and that the corporation had a wonderful pension scheme, she saw a vision of herself in Gainham Woods forever, seeing the same people, being driven in Tess every other Sunday to see Don's father and mother, going to the pictures once a week, having sex once a month, going in Tess to an English seaside resort for a holiday once a year. The car seemed the symbol of this terrible routine.

'When shall we get rid of that car?'

'Tess? She may need a new battery soon, but she's running beautifully now I've tuned up the engine.'

'Shall we still have her when you're pensioned off? Perhaps she'll outlive us and come to the funeral.' She began to laugh on a high note.

'If that's meant to be funny, I think it's a very poor joke.'

A few weeks later Moira had a letter from a solicitor telling her that her father had died out in New Zealand. It seemed that he had done rather well out there, and although he had married the woman he went off with and she got most of his money, he had remembered Moira in his will to the tune of several thousands.

She spoke to Don again about moving, saying that they could use her money as deposit on a new house. He positively refused. It was her money, and he wouldn't think of using it for any such purpose.

'After all, I'm the breadwinner, my dear, and that's how it should be. I'm quite able to support us both.'

He had taken to calling her 'my dear' lately, but she did not say how middle-aged it made her feel, or how much it irritated her.

'Couldn't we at least use the money, some of the money, to get another car? A new one.'

His mouth turned down in the expression that she had once thought conveyed strength of character. Now it just seemed to her to show weak, pouting obstinacy.

'I shouldn't think of getting rid of Tess.'

'I could buy a car of my own.'

He looked at her in astonishment. 'Where should we keep it? I couldn't turn Tess out of the garage. And anyway, my dear, your driving –'

He did not finish the sentence. It was on the tip of her tongue to say that she had passed the test with flying colours, but what was the use? It was true they only had a one-car garage, and if she bought a car it would not be allowed to stand in the road.

So she said nothing further. Don read all the financial columns to discover the safest forms of investment, and consulted Mr Bradbury who advised putting the inheritance into National Savings. It stayed on deposit in the bank.

Twice a year Don went away on group study courses to which the corporation sent their personnel officers. The courses lasted five days, and it was during one of his absences that she went to Marjorie Allenden's party. Marjorie had been to school with Moira, and they had met in a department store when Moira went up to London to do some shopping. Marjorie worked on a fashion magazine and was married to Clive, who worked in some editorial capacity on a glossy weekly.

The Allendens had a flat just off Earl's Court Road. It was furnished with brightly coloured sofas and eccentrically shaped chairs. There were lots of paintings on the walls, most of them abstracts. Moira was very impressed. It was just the kind of place she would have liked, although she did not say so. The mantelpiece was quite bare except for a large Victorian teapot, and Marjorie drew the attention of all her visitors to this.

'Clive picked it up in the Portobello Road for thirty bob,' she said in the high emphatic voice she seemed to have acquired. 'Don't you think it's too fascinatingly hideous?'

'Just hideous,' A voice behind Moira murmured. It

belonged to a dark young man of about her own age who wore narrow light-blue trousers, a dark-blue jersey, and the small gold-rimmed spectacles that she knew were the latest thing. When he smiled at her she smiled back.

His name was Louis and he was a partner in a photographic agency. While they drank some kind of rather potent reddish liquid they talked – rather, he talked and she listened. Through the hum of noise she heard that he was an American who had been in London for two years now, and wasn't going back.

'I've always wanted to go to New York,' she said.

'Beside London it's just dead, baby.'

'It's not your scene,' she ventured. It was a word she had often heard used by young people on television; but perhaps she used it wrongly, because he laughed.

'You're wonderful.' He looked at her through those fascinating little gold-rimmed glasses. 'Look, this is strictly from Deadsville. What do you say we get out of here and eat? I know a nice little place.'

His car was parked just outside the house, ignoring the forbidding double yellow lines, and she gasped when she saw it. It was long, sleek, low and immensely wide, and seemed to be totally enclosed in glass. When she ducked down into the passenger seat she had the double feeling of being almost on the ground because the car was so low, and of being on the bridge of a ship with total visibility all round her. He dropped into the seat beside her, gunned the engine, and she felt the exciting surge of power as they drove away.

She asked what make of car it was and he said casually it was Italian, a Ghiani-Lucia, a make she had never heard of. 'Felix Ghiani's a friend of mine, asked me to try it out.'

They reached the restaurant and she felt that people were looking at her as they got out of the gleaming monster. Louis was known, a doorman rushed forward to greet him, and inside the restaurant everybody knew him; the head waiter left another table to come over and shake hands.

Afterwards she tried to remember what they ate and drank, but although she clearly recalled the long menu and could even see the mauve ink in which it was written, she had not the faintest recollection of any of the dishes or the wines. But she could afterwards remember talking about herself, about Don and the boredom of life in Gainham Woods, and possibly – she was not quite sure of this – about her hatred of Tess.

Once or twice she had caught him looking at her through his gold rims with a speculative gaze, as though she were a creature of some new species to whom he was giving coolly sympathetic consideration. At the end of the meal he said, 'Coffee at my pad, as you cool young hipsters put it?'

'You're laughing at me,' she said happily. She longed to be back inside the Ghiani-Lucia, to feel the exhilarating movement of it beneath her.

The drive was all that she had expected and when they reached his flat she was a little drunk, just enough to make the outlines of everything seem faintly hazy – but not so drunk that she failed to look forward with excitement to the prospect of making love. Yet in the end the exciting prospect turned into something rather dismayingly practical and even disappointing when he said that he thought every woman should remember the Boy Scouts' motto, 'Be Prepared', before going to a party, and then seemed to take for granted a great deal that was strange and uncongenial to her. Afterwards she looked at his dark hairy body, thought of the clean metallic power within the Ghiani-Lucia, and shuddered slightly. At the same time it occurred to her that Don might phone home, and she was suddenly eager to be back.

'Okay, I'll ring for a taxi.' She had hoped he would take her in the car, but did not say so. 'I'd take you myself, but it's been a hard day.'

'It's not very far.' She wanted very much to ride in the car again.

His gaze was mocking. 'Gainham Woods? Baby, I've never been that far in my life.'

On the way back she cried, although she could not have said exactly why. The taxi took her home and she paid the man off at the end of the road. In the house she looked at everything as though it belonged to a stranger, then went out into the garage, turned on the light, and stared at the dull black car. Don did not phone.

She telephoned Louis the next day, not because she particularly wanted to see him, but because she wanted to experience again the excitement she had felt in the car. He said that he was going out of town and wasn't sure when he would be back. 'Don't call me, baby, I'll call you,' he said. She put down the phone without saying goodbye.

Two days later, on Friday night, Don returned. The group study course had been pretty exhausting, he said, had anything happened in his absence? Yes, she said, she had something to tell him. She showed him her driver's licence and he was as surprised as she had expected. He agreed that she could drive Tess, but she sensed his lack of enthusiasm.

On Saturday morning she sat in the driver's seat. But Tess would not start.

Don had the hood up in a flash, but soon closed it. 'Battery's almost dead. Perhaps if I push her out she might start. You guide her.'

She nodded. It was a small garage and he had to squeeze round to get between the car and the rear wall. The gleaming row of garden instruments was directly behind him. He levered himself against the wall and pushed the car ahead of him two or three yards, then indicated that she should try again to start it. She turned the ignition and the motor came to life.

Don raised a thumb. 'Good old girl. Now back her out.'

She put the car into reverse (as she explained to a sympathetic coroner at the inquest) and released the clutch. But it moved forward instead of back. She lost her head, tried to brake, instead pushed the accelerator harder, and then. . .

The sympathetic coroner spared her the necessity of going on. Don was standing directly in front of the rake. He was transfixed by the sharp new tines like a piece of bread on a toasting fork. But if the rake had not been there, the coroner said consolingly, he would undoubtedly have been crushed to death against the wall.

An expert motor-car engineer gave evidence. He said that the car was very old and badly needed new gears. You hardly needed to depress the clutch to move from one gear to another. It was the easiest thing in the world to slip into first instead of reverse.

Friends and neighbours were very sympathetic, like the coroner. Don Bradbury had made himself known and respected in Gainham Woods, and indeed they were a most devoted couple. 'He was a real member of our community,' the vicar said to Moira at the funeral.

Afterwards she got rid of Tess. As she explained to Marjorie Allenden, she couldn't keep a car that had killed her husband. It was Marjorie who helped her to find a nice little flat in Camden Town, which at least wasn't in the heart of deadly exurbia like Gainham Woods.

A week after moving in she bought a Ghiani-Lucia.

The Best Chess Player in the World

'All I ask is value for money,' George Bernard Shaw said.

The man on the other side of the desk, whose name was Roberts, shuffled his feet and looked miserable.

Shaw had been given those first names by his parents, because it was on the night of a visit to *Arms and the Man* that he had been conceived. Others might have flinched from the names, but he had accepted them even at school, and for years now had taken pleasure in using the full name, or for preference the magic initials. He regarded himself as a disciple of the original George Bernard Shaw, who in his eyes had not been a visonary socialist but a ruthless realist, fighting battles in his dealings with theatre producers, publishers, women, battles which he always won. The original Shaw had been, as he saw it, a man with cranky ideas which he cleverly exploited in plays to make himself a lot of money. In life, however, he had been a logical man, and the later GBS prided himself on being logical too.

He was twenty-five when he inherited from his father a small family printing firm and a couple of weekly local papers. The local papers were now a flourishing chain of thirty, that covered the Midlands and extended up into Yorkshire and Lancashire. The printing works had enlarged with the papers.

Success had not been achieved without some difficulties, as is the way of life. There had been problems with wholesalers in some areas, people who complained that GBS gave much poorer terms than his competitors, and so refused to stock his papers. These wholesalers found their vans damaged through slashed tyres, sand in the tank, and other means. Their warehouses also suffered burglaries, in which stock was damaged or destroyed. Such difficulties ceased when they handled, and pushed, GBS papers.

Then there were union problems at the works. GBS always refused to employ union members, and the local branches threatened to black him. The two union secretaries who had led the blacking movement were badly beaten up, one sustaining several broken ribs and the other a hip injury that left him permanently lame. Half a dozen other militants suffered similar, although less severe attacks, and eventually GBS's firm was left alone. He was the ruler of his world, and the feeling was enjoyable. The interview with Roberts took place because it was understood that GBS was the last court of appeal. Roberts, when sacked, had gone to the top man.

'Value for money,' GBS said. 'And from the reports on the table here I'm not getting it.'

'I've been here more than twenty years.'

'Twenty-two. What then?'

'Now I'm to be turned off with a month's notice.'

'You feel you are being badly treated? Let us consider.' There was nothing he enjoyed more than an argument of this kind, in which he held all the trump cards. 'You came here and stayed here of your own free will. You worked as a packer and a machine hand, jobs that required no tradesman's skills, but still you were paid more than you would have been in a union shop. Your job, however, while involving no special skill, did demand that you should stand up at work. You tell me this is impossible –'

'It's my leg, my arthritis. You'd never believe the pain. The specialist, he says I must sit down, not all day, I got to keep moving, but just sit down sometimes, every half hour. Standing's the worst thing for it, standing all day.' Roberts was a small man with a drooping moustache. He spoke with the nasal whine of the area.

'Then of course you must sit down. But that means you are unable to do your job here.'

'I'm being thrown on the scrapheap. No pension, nothing.'

'You knew there was no pension scheme when you came –'

'I was young then, never thought about it.'

'Please do not interrupt. You should have thought, you should have saved money. Now you must look for another job.'

'With my leg, and me forty-seven years old, and unemployment what it is, what chance have I got? You could find me another job here, something behind a desk, easy enough if you wanted.'

GBS never ceased to be polite, but now he allowed his impatience to show. 'Why should I do that? The reports I have here don't suggest that you would be able to handle such work. You have never worked behind a desk, you would be useless, and we are not a charity. You must be logical, Mr Roberts. Value for money is the rule between employer and employed. If you felt you were worth more than we paid you, you were free to take another job. Now you are no longer giving value for money. What more is there to say?'

Roberts found other things to say, abusive and illogical things to which GBS paid no attention. He would not have admitted even to himself that he enjoyed such interviews, but he always found pleasure in pointing out that the value for money argument was irrefutable. The pleasure lasted during half of the forty minute drive home. Then he began to think about Paula.

He had married Paula ten years ago, when he was thirty-five and she ten years younger. For some time he had felt no need to marry. He had a flat in the heart of the city, and when it was necessary to entertain for business purposes, a local firm sent in an excellent cook, and a maid to serve the meal. Then he had interests, apart from the firm, that kept him busy. He acknowledged the need to keep fit, and like his namesake was a useful boxer. Games seemed to him ridiculous, but he understood that they could be useful in business terms, and made himself into an efficient golfer, particularly on the greens, since putting seemed to him the most logical part of the game. He went often to race meetings, where he was a heavy punter. Was that illogical? Not so, for his bets were in the service of the Emergency Fund. When he won he was paid in cash, and the money went straight into a safe deposit account in London. This was the Emergency Fund. It had been used on several occasions when the use of cheques would have been inadvisable.

He acknowledged also the need for sex. He took girls out, sometimes for a day at the races, sometimes for dinner. Either way they ended up in bed at the flat, a result he felt essential to justify the time and money spent. A time came, however, when to his own surprise he found all this unsatisfactory. He felt the need for a house of his own, for somebody to arrange those dinners, and to sit at one end of the table. A number of business acquaintances raised their eyebrows when they found that there was no hostess at his dinners, and he knew that there were always whispers about bachelors. Then again, a good deal of trouble in the sexual line would be saved if he had a wife. It would be a practical arrangement, she would be value for money. The right kind of wife, of course, somebody who looked on marriage as logically as he did himself.

He met Paula Mountford at a party, asked her to dinner and to the theatre, but made no attempt to take her to bed. He decided that she filled the bill perfectly. She was the younger daughter of a county family that had come down in the world, good-looking enough in a slightly awkward, big-boned way, and adept in keeping her conversational end up in any sort of company. She was also a girl with an eye on the main chance, something that was evident when he took her back to the flat, kissed her, and suggested that they should get married.

'You aren't in love with me.'

'I don't talk about love, it's an abstraction. I find you attractive, and we seem to get on well.'

'Well enough,' she said coolly. She had a thick underlip, and it was stuck out now. 'I don't love you, I'm not sure that I like you very much, but you're certain of yourself, you go out for what you want, and I admire that. At the moment you seem to want me. I suppose I should be flattered.'

'I'm glad you're sensible.'

'Not much use being anything else when you're around,' she said with a laugh.

'I've got no time for romance, it seems to me nonsense. I think you should consider whether the advantages of being married to me are enough for you.'

'All right. I'll tell you what I want. A wedding in style, church not registry office, no expense spared. A house outside the city, I hate bricks and mortar all round me. An acre or so of garden. My own car, a runabout. A couple of horses, I want to keep up my hunting. Good for your image to have a wife who hunts. A big dog, retriever or a labrador. A clothes account up in London, no complaints about how much I spend. That's all at the moment, though I shall think of other things I'm sure. In return I'll grace your table and share your bed. I don't suppose you want children?' He shook his head. 'Luckily I'm not mad about them either.'

'We agree about everything. It sounds as though you're good value for money.' He smiled as he said it, but the words were serious.

'My God, you are a bastard.' She pulled him to her. He was surprised, and disconcerted, by the ardency of her embrace.

Three months later Paula Mountford became Mrs George Bernard Shaw.

For years the arrangement had, it seemed to him, worked perfectly. Paula had everything she wanted. She had chosen the house, a large modern villa out in the country with a lot of ground, and outbuildings that were converted into a stable block. She had her horses, her golden retriever. She proved to be an excellent hostess, inventive with menus, skilful in making nervous guests feel at ease. She dressed individually and with flair, and he never said a word about bills. As for sex that rather lapsed, as he felt by mutual consent. He no longer felt much need for it, and the exercise of power in the firm was something that he found much more exciting. The firm prospered, his home life prospered. He was a contented man.

Until the day when he learned that Paula had a lover.

He learned it in the simplest way. He had mislaid his cigarette lighter, looked in an old bag of hers in the hope of finding one, and there was the letter. He was an incurious man, and would not have read it except that the word 'Darling' caught his eye. The words on the page seemed to him hardly credible. Could it be Paula to whom these phrases were addressed, embarrassing and ridiculous phrases of a kind that he would never have been able to bring himself to put down on paper? Paula was up in London, and it was typical of him that his first action after making the discovery was to go on looking for a light, and then to smoke his cigarette before reading the letter again.

He congratulated himself on this calmness, but it was succeeded by a wave of anger such as he had never known. The anger had no outward manifestation, he did not break any of Paula's possessions or cut up her clothes, but the emotion shook him as he had not been shaken since he was eleven years old. He had been told then by his father that his mother had left the house forever, and gone to live with another man. He had felt that as a personal betrayal, a possession he had lost, and now he felt the same thing. Paula belonged to him, he had given her everything she ever asked for, and she had now deliberately betrayed him. She must be punished.

He made a copy of the letter, and returned it to the bag. It was, again, typical of him that he did not consider asking the name of her lover, or whether the affair was over. Such questions might lead to argument, and he only argued from a position of assured superiority. Should he employ a private detective? He decided against this, partly because it was Paula's betrayal that concerned him and not the name of her past or present lover, but principally for the reason that to consult a private detective involved putting himself to some extent in the man's power, and to put himself in somebody else's power was something that he had never done in his life. Instead he watched Paula himself, following her by car on the days when she said that she would be going out. He did not use his own car, which she might have recognised, but rented one. In less than a week he had discovered the identity of her lover. He was a man of Paula's own age, divorced from his wife, a well-to-do gentleman farmer who was a member of the hunt she rode with. The man lived a few miles away, and she went to his house one or two afternoons a week.

But GBS was little interested in the man, and did not blame him. He appreciated that to sleep with another man's wife was a kind of triumph, one he had savoured himself in his bachelor days, when the chief pleasure had been talking afterwards to the unwitting cuckold. It was

Paula who must be punished, but it was easier to say this than to discover the means. He did not threaten divorce, because he feared that this would be no punishment, and also it would mean that she was no longer in his possession. What else could he do that would make her miserable as she deserved to be miserable, take away forever that look of a cat almost choked with cream that he now saw on her face? He thought about it for days while the anger grew within him, grew satisfyingly because he knew that it would find an outlet. Eventually he decided that the only possible punishment was death.

It was necessary to assure himself that the punishment was just, and this was not difficult. Look at the matter logically, and it was apparent that he and Paula had an agreement. She had broken it, and no longer gave value for the money she received. It was true, and he acknowledged it, that the idea of her suffering pleased him, as he had been pleased by the lasting nature of the injuries sustained by that trade union branch secretary. He considered, and reluctantly rejected, the idea that Paula's horse face might be permanently scarred. What would happen afterwards? He could hardly divorce her without incurring blame, and he had no wish to spend the rest of his life with a disfigured woman.

He was aware that the logic he used was that of a superior man (in a phrase, the logic of GBS), and that it would not be generally understood. In the event of Paula's death he would be an obvious suspect, and he had no intention of standing in a dock, or even suffering arrest. It was essential therefore that he should not have any apparent connection with what happened. He would work through intermediaries, but none of them must see him, or be able to make a connection leading back to him. It was a difficult problem, but one of an intellectual kind, resembling a problem in chess. He played chess well, and in a day or two he had solved the problem.

The first person to see was Jerry Wilde. Jerry owed him a debt, but he would not rely on that. The logical man does not depend on emotion.

The debts Jerry owed him, for they were counted in the plural, went back to their days at grammar school. GBS had always been, like his namesake, long and wiry, physically capable of looking after himself. Jerry Wilde was the kind of perky little shrimp who was a natural target for bullying. It had been amusing to defend him, and to show his contempt for the rest of the school by making it clear that he would sooner talk to Jerry than to the captain of cricket. Jerry's worshipful attitude, his readiness to run errands and in general to do what he was told, were also agreeable. He was a lively little boy, an excellent mimic, good especially at catching the tones of other boys, and a great success in the school plays. But there was a basic dishonesty about Jerry. He would cheat in exams even though he knew the answers, and GBS had once saved him from the threat of expulsion for stealing, by pretending to find the missing money, which he had provided out of his own pocket.

Jerry's later career was much what might have been predicted. He got jobs but couldn't hold them. He went on benders and failed to turn up for work, fiddled accounts when he had anything to do with money, was always ready to help in handling TV sets, cases of whisky, or other quickly saleable things without asking where they came from. GBS had saved him from an embezzlement charge by paying his employer something over the amount Jerry had taken, and from something more serious when Jerry, blind drunk at the wheel of a car, had mounted the pavement and knocked down an old age pensioner. She had been persuaded to take money instead of pressing charges. Why did he bother with Jerry? Well, on both those occasions he had made Jerry sign a statement admitting the facts. And then Jerry seemed to know or be able to get the dirt on everybody, and GBS had made use of this knowledge. It was Jerry who had found the boys who turned the trick with the vans and those who tamed the trade unionists, who told them what to do and paid them off, so that GBS never even knew who they were. Jerry was useful.

At the moment he was working for a man who cannibalised cars, put bits and pieces into other cars that had been in accidents and sold for scrap. Then he sprayed them, changed the speedo and plates, and sold them as salesman's models.

'Looking for a car, boss? Give you a good trade in on the one you've got.' Jerry had always been a grinner. Above the grin his nose was bright red with alcohol, his cheeks hardly less so.

'I wanted a chat.'

'Round at the King's Head?' GBS shook his head, made a gesture towards his car. 'Like that, is it? Mind the shop Bill, shan't be long.' Bill, at the back of the showroom, waved a hand. They drove a couple of miles, then GBS pulled into a lay-by.

'You're going to land in trouble with those cars,' he said. 'The registration plate on that Jaguar, where did it come from?'

'Couldn't tell you off-hand.'

'And what about the registration book?'

'Looks beautiful. Don't ask where I got it, not unless you're a buyer.'

'You won't get away with it for long.'

'And when there's trouble who shall I run to? Don't tell me. Did we come out here for you to say that, or just to look at the traffic?'

'Neither. I need a little help.'

Jerry cocked his head to one side, bird-like. 'Yours to command.'

'It's a little bit like the Layton business.' Layton had sustained the hip injury.

'And you want me to find a couple of boys, fix it with them?'

'Not exactly. I want somebody reliable, very reliable. You find him, give me a number where I can call him. You don't, not on any account, mention my name. That's it.'

'That's it?' Jerry's bright bird eye showed surprise. 'You'll handle it yourself? Why and wherefore?'

'Not your business. You just give me a name and number.'

'The boss orders, it shall be done.' He sketched a salute. 'A bit ticklish though. The sort of boy I know, he knows me. But he *don't* know you, if you get my meaning. If I knew the strength of what you wanted, that would help.'

'No. It's better to stick to what I said.'

'That means it must be strong.'

He affected irritation. 'If you don't want to help, say so. There'd be fifty pounds in it for you, just for a name and number.'

'When have I ever said no? It's ticklish, that's all. I might have to put you on to somebody who'd pass you on, get me? Leave it with me for a day or two, I'll ask around. Discreetly mind, don't worry. That's it?'

'That's it.'

'Then let's get back.' When they were back at the showroom Jerry stuck his head through the car window. His breath smelt of beer and pickled onions. 'About the fifty, GBS, forget it. This one's on the house.'

Two days later he rang back with a name and number. 'Like I said, it's someone who'll make the arrangements. Can't say more, he'll tell you the rest himself. Say you're a friend of mine when you call. Ring at five o'clock any afternoon, he'll be there. And, boss?'

'Yes?'

'Be careful. They're wide awake, some of these boys.'

The thought of the dangerous element involved made his blood tingle, his heart beat pleasurably faster. The danger of involvement was part of the game, its avoidance a mark of the logician's skill. Had Jerry understood that? In any case his part was now finished, and he could say nothing damaging.

He rang the number from a public call box just after five o'clock. The voice that came on was low, cautious.

'Is that Mr Middleton, Jack Middleton?'

'Yes.'

'Jerry Wilde gave me your name, said I could call you.'

'Jerry, right.'

'He thought you might be able to help me with a problem.'

'What sort of problem?'

'A friend of mine needs a job done.'

Now the voice rose a little, roughened, a voice definitely not out of the top drawer.

'I don't know what you're talking about. Who are you, what's your name?'

'My friend wants me to remain private.'

'Is that so? You just tell him my name's Jack Middleton and I like to know who I'm dealing with. Got it?'

'Yes. Don't hang up, Mr Middleton. We're talking about a big job, a lot of money.'

Silence. 'How much is a lot? And what's it for?'

'My friend wants –' He found, quite unexpectedly, that he could not form the words. He was strongly conscious of the interior of the telephone box. On one wall somebody had written *Tony loves Lucy* and on another *United Rule OK?*.

The harsh voice said, 'What's up? Want somebody hit,

is that it?'

Hit, did that mean killed? He was not sure. 'Disposed of.' The words came out choked, as if he was being strangled.

'Say it how you like. Ten grand.'

'*How* much?'

'Ten grand. That covers it, my commission included.'

He was so astonished that he was briefly silent. He wanted to expostulate, to say that the jobs done before had cost no more than a few hundred, but very likely Middleton knew nothing about them. When he found his voice he said, 'That's much more than my friend expected. It's too much.'

'Please yourself. That's the price.'

'I must – must consult. I take it nothing would be payable until –'

'Half in advance, other half when it's done.'

'But that would be trusting you with five thousand pounds.'

'Who's trusting who, mister?' the coarse voice asked. 'I don't even know your bloody name.'

He left the box a little shaken. He was so used to being in a position of mastery, to dealing with everybody as he had dealt with Roberts, that to be almost in the position of a supplicant was disconcerting. Perhaps he should give up the whole thing, tell Paula that he knew of her affair and threaten to cut off her allowance and stop her charge accounts? But supposing she ignored him, supposing she went off to live with her gentleman farmer and made him a laughing stock? Even the possibility was not to be contemplated.

That weekend they gave a dinner party. The food was delicious, Paula as usual an admirable hostess, but he felt half a dozen times during the evening that she was mocking him. When the guests had gone he felt such a wave of fury that he could have strangled her, or shot her with the old Webley that he had inherited from his father, who had fancied himself as a shot and had set up a target in the back garden. In fact the revolver was in his desk drawer and they were talking in the bedroom, so that the question of such a spontaneous action did not arise. In any event it would of course have been stupid, illogical, unworthy of GBS. But that evening made him decide to go ahead. On Monday evening he rang Middleton again, calling as he had been told to do at five o'clock.

'I've talked to my friend. He'd like to go ahead. On the lines you mentioned.'

'What's his name? Your *friend*, I mean.'

'No names. That's a condition.'

'All right.' There was an unexpected chuckle. 'But there's one name you gotta give me, what you might call the subject.' GBS gave Paula's name, and their address. 'You never said it was a woman.'

He replied with a touch of his usual acerbity. 'Before we were just talking. Now it's serious, and there things I want to know. Is your agent reliable? Does it make any difference to him that it's a woman?'

'Makes no odds to him, it's just a job. He was one of those what you call 'em, mercenaries, out in Angola, free-lance now. You can talk to him yourself, make up your own mind.'

'I don't want to meet him.'

'You don't have to. I said talk, not meet. I'll give you a number to ring, ask for Charlie.'

'About making payment –'

'Talk to Charlie. You fix it with him, you pay him, he gives me my cut. He knows there might be a job, so just mention me. Here's the number.' He gave it. 'Just one thing, he ain't always there. I'd call in the evening, between six and eight. After eight he's usually out with the boys.'

'He's reliable, he wouldn't talk about it to them?'

'He's a professional.'

The first time he rang the number there was no reply. The second time a voice answered, and said it was Charlie.

'I've been put on to you by Jack Middleton. About a job I want done.'

'Jack said something, gave me the name. And you're Mr X, incognito you might call it.' The voice had a disagreeable twang to it, some accent he could not place. Was it South African? Charlie began asking practical questions. When did he want it done? As soon as possible. GBS had given some thought to the method, and said that if it could look like a car accident, that would be ideal. Charlie said a decisive no to that, as too hard to arrange. Then an attempted burglary of the house, the subject came home unexpectedly –

The voice with its odd twang interrupted. 'You've been reading too many books, Mr X. First thing I look after is Number One. It's got to be simple, probably at night, a gun with a silencer. If I can make it look like a robbery okay, but don't rely on it. Don't rely on anything, except the job being done.'

'When?'

'Give me a week after I've got the first instalment. Let's talk about that. I want used notes, ones and fives. You drop it by a rubbish bin on the London road, I pick it up, I'll give you the details.'

'No.'

For the first time the voice lost its assurance. 'What you mean, no?'

'That won't do. You could check on my car or see me. You said I'm incognito. I want to stay that way. Now, this is what I propose.'

Charlie listened, then said, 'And the other five? When the job's done?'

'The same way.'

'Fancy but clever. Think of everything, Mr X, don't you?'

'I try to.' Then they discussed the timing.

The conversation took place on Monday evening. On Wednesday afternoon GBS took the 2.30 train out of the city. It was a slow train that stopped at several places, and it was busy during the rush hours but two-thirds empty in the afternoons, so that he had no trouble in finding a carriage to himself.

When he was a boy they had lived at Thelsby, almost at the end of the line, and he had travelled hundreds of times on the train to school. A couple of miles before Thelsby there was a stretch of single-track line, and the train from the city always stopped to let one from the other direction come through. At the point where it stopped there was a grass embankment to one side, and often in that distant past he and Jerry had jumped out of the carriage, half-run and half-rolled down the grass, leapt down the steep bank at the end, and wriggled through the wire that separated the embankment from the road.

Today the train stopped as it had always done. GBS muffled his face in a scarf. There was a whistle, the train for the city passed them. He opened the carriage window. Their own train began to move, very slowly. He flung the cheap attache case as far as he could down the grass slope. He could see no sign of Charlie, who was no doubt concealed behind the steep drop at the bottom. All Charlie could have seen of him was a hand, and a face hidden behind a scarf. On the way back from Thelsby he looked out to where he had thrown the attache case, and saw only grass.

It was perfect.

He recited the perfection of it to himself all the way home. It was inevitable that after Paula's death all three people involved, Jerry, Jack and Charlie, should assume that he had ordered it. Let them think so, for they could prove nothing. And what could the police prove? If they talked to Jerry, any admission he made would be damaging to himself, and so could be ruled out. As for Jack Middleton and Charlie, what identification could they make beyond a voice on the telephone?

Of course he would be a suspect. He was prepared for long interrogations, and even looked forward to them because he knew that he would emerge triumphant. No doubt the police would discover the gentleman farmer, but this revelation would come as a total surprise to GBS. (How wise he had been not to use a private detective.) And the police would look in vain for any discrepancies in his bank account, or any large withdrawals, for the money had come from the Emergency Fund. Would he pay the rest of the money after the job was done? He kept an open mind about it, feeling that it must be possible to make some deal with Charlie.

It was a logical operation, and in such an operation every possibility is taken into account, so that the unexpected cannot occur. He had only to sit back and await the result.

Thursday passed, and Friday. He drove into the works as usual, chaired editorial discussions, had talks with a consortium that was talking about making an offer for two of his weeklies. While he went about these occupations he waited for the telephone call, or for the policeman who would begin: 'I'm sorry to say, Mr Shaw, that. . .' On Friday afternoon, he knew, Paula saw her farmer. Perhaps while she was driving home. . . or when she returned to the house . . ?

But when he returned on Friday he was greeted by the

smell of boeuf bourguignon and found Paula in the kitchen, making a first course of avocado and prawns. She had the *sleek* look she always wore after a session with her lover, a look that dissipated any possible feeling of regret. On Saturday Paula went out with the hunt, on Sunday morning the papers were late and she drove down to the village to get them. Each time he wound himself up into a state of expectation, but nothing happened. On Sunday evening he was unable to sit still to watch TV, made an excuse and went to his study, where he sat at his desk staring out into the dark night. When he returned she was watching a gangster series.

On Monday morning she said that she was going to London. Whether she did so, or saw her farmer, she was at home in the evening.

On Tuesday nothing happened.

Give me a week after I've got the first instalment. On Wednesday afternoon the week was up. And on that evening Paula came home in the best of spirits after, as she said, an afternoon spent with a couple of girl friends. They were giving a dinner party on Friday, and she had done some shopping for it.

On Thursday morning he left home as usual, went to a call box and rang Charlie's number. No reply. He drove in to the works, dealt with correspondence, went out twice to call boxes. The number rang, but there was no answer. Ring between six and eight in the evening, Jack Middleton had said. He rang at six with no result, and then called the exchange to ask if the line was in working order. In less than a minute the operator came back to him.

'That number is a public call box.'

'*What?* It isn't possible. There must be a mistake.'

'I will repeat the number,' the operator said, and did so. 'Is that correct? Very good. That is the number of a public call box.'

He asked where it was, and was given the name of a street in the east end of the city. He drove down there, looked at the red glass-windowed box, even went into it as though there might be an answer to his questions within. In some way or other he had been cheated, either by Charlie or by Jack Middleton. He did not ring Middleton, but went to see Jerry Wilde.

Jerry was in the King's Head, drinking what was obviously not his first or second brandy and soda. He greeted GBS with a slap on the back, and asked how things were going.

'I have to talk to you. Come out now. Right away.'

'Can't be done, boss. Got to meet a man about a car. Big deal. Be here any minute. Then taking him out for a drive, back here, have a couple of drinks, argue the toss about the price –'

It might just have been possible to talk sense to Jerry now, but in an hour or two it would be useless to try.

'Come and see me tomorrow.'

'Anything you say. When and where?'

On Friday there was a meeting at the office which was likely to take all day. He told Jerry to come to the house at six o'clock. He would be gone long before seven thirty, when the dinner party guests arrived.

'Unexpected honour, boss. I'll be there.' It was true that Jerry was not the kind of person he asked home, and that Paula did not care for him, but the circumstances were exceptional.

On Friday, punctually at six, Jerry drove up in a Jaguar, no doubt the one with the fake registration book. He wore a hat with a little feather in it, and a check suit. Paula was passing through the hall on the way to the kitchen when he arrived, and greeted him coolly. After that they went to the study. GBS sat behind his desk and told Jerry what had happened. At the end he said, 'I want an explanation.'

Jerry wriggled. 'You know what you sound like? Old Porson, our old head. *I want an explanation, Wilde.* And I knew I'd never be able to explain, not to his satisfaction. You wouldn't have a drink handy?'

'After the explanation.'

'I only put you in touch with Jack Middleton. Have you tried ringing him?'

'No. It was Charlie who arranged to take the money.'

'Trouble is I don't know Charlie, do I? Why not try Jack, see what he's got to say? Here, I'll dial the number for you, I know it.' He did so, and held up the receiver so that GBS could hear the ringing tone. Then he dialled again.

'What are you doing?'

'Just checking. Operator, will you run a check on one-eight-three-four-six. I've been dialling, and can't get a reply. What's that, what do you say? Well I never. Many thanks.' He put down the telephone, grinned. 'Would you believe it, that's a public call box.'

'But that isn't possible. You put me in touch with Middleton.'

'That's right.'

'You must know him.'

'Right again, boss, I know him.' Out of Jerry Wilde's grinning face came the rough voice. *'You just tell him my name's Jack Middleton.* I know Charlie too.' And GBS heard again that disagreeable twang. *'You've been reading too many stories, Mr X. The first thing I look after is Number One.* I was always able to manage voices, remember?'

Even now he could not believe it. 'The attache case. It was you who collected it.'

'Nobody else. I thought it was a nice touch, dropping it where we used to scramble down as kids. Sentimental. Nearly piped my eye.'

'You've robbed me, stolen five thousand pounds.'

Jerry's grin became a laugh. 'I don't see it that way. I

reckon you owe it me.'

'But I've always helped you. I kept you out of prison.'

'And made me sign statements so that you could hold 'em over me. Only you can't use 'em now, can you, or you'd have to say why you hung on to them so long. Did you think I liked being an errand boy? Anyway, the answer's no. So when you were so mysterious I thought, well, let's see just what he's got in mind, shall we. And my word, wasn't it naughty?' Jerry wiped his red face with a handkerchief, and went on.

'I wouldn't try again to do something naughty about your wife, because I might have something interesting to tell the fuzz. And you can't do anything about the five thousand, can you, *boss?* I'm taking a holiday for a few weeks, can't make up my mind whether it's Madeira or the West Indies, but before I went I wanted to see your face when I told you. Incidentally, I bet you meant to cheat poor old Charlie out of his second five grand. Do you know where I'd say you are, boss? Up the creek without a paddle.'

Before this speech was half-way through, George Bernard Shaw had ceased to be a logical and reasonable man, and had become a machine filled with nothing but hatred for the creature opposite him. He acted not reasonably, but from this uncontrollable hatred when he opened the right hand drawer of the desk, took out the revolver, and shot Jerry Wilde neatly between the eyes.

George Bernard Shaw went to Broadmoor. There he became the chess champion, and every month composed a chess problem which he sent to the world champion, challenging him to solve it. From the fact that he never received any reply to these communications he made the logical deduction that the champion was unable to solve the problems, and by the extension of this logic that George Bernard Shaw was the best chess player in the world.

MORE ABOUT PENGUINS, PELICANS AND PUFFINS

JULIAN SYMONS

A selection

THE BLACKHEATH POISONINGS

'A superb detective novel of an original kind, which, while offering the reader as much information as anyone, ends with a surprising and totally unexpected conclusion. At the same time his evocation of this late Victorian epoch – a kind of black *Diary of a Nobody* – seems to ring true in every respect' – *The Times Literary Supplement*

THE TELL-TALE HEART

THE LIFE AND WORKS OF EDGAR ALLAN POE

'Mr Symon's analysis of Poe's divided self is uncondescending, and does not simplify his subject. On the contrary, he rescues Poe from Freudians, symbolists, moralists and other simplifiers. By indicating the ramifications of the two selves, he restores to Poe his depth and mystery. He manages to be both incisive and finely circumspect . . . And he even makes you like Poe most of the time' – John Carey in the *Sunday Times*